LET ALL THE CLOCKS RUN DOWN!

Twist Time, intertwine it with Space, wrap the scintillating ribbon round your finger and wish you were in **Cinnabar.**

Leap light years and land on both feet in the midst of an incredible company which would have staggered the imagination of H. G. Wells or Jules Verne.

Grab tight hold of the seatbelt of whirling conceptions, transversing infinite parsecs and millennia . . . let this marvelously imagined novel be your passport to the city at the center of time . . .

CINNABAR

CINNABAR

Edward Bryant

BANTAM BOOKS · TORONTO · NEW YORK · LONDON

This one is for the members of the Denver
and Colorado Springs SF Writers' Workshops;
but is especially for Doris Beetem the Elder,
first honorary citizen of Cinnabar.

*This low-priced Bantam Book
has been completely reset in a type face
designed for easy reading, and was printed
from new plates. It contains the complete
text of the original hard-cover edition.*
NOT ONE WORD HAS BEEN OMITTED.

CINNABAR

*A Bantam Book / published by arrangement with
Macmillan Publishing Company, Inc.*

PRINTING HISTORY
*Macmillan edition published August 1976
Bantam edition / August 1977*

Acknowledgments

The Road to Cinnabar, Copyright © 1971 by Lancer Books, Inc. Originally appeared in *Infinity*.

Jade Blue, Copyright © 1971 by Terry Carr. Originally appeared in *Universe*.

Gray Matters (as *Their Thousandth Season*), Copyright © 1972 by Edward Bryant. Originally appeared in *Clarion*. Also appeared in *Among the Dead*, Macmillan, 1973.

The Legend of Cougar Lou Landis, Copyright © 1973 by Terry Carr. Originally appeared in *Universe*.

Hayes and the Heterogyne, Copyright © 1974 by Mankind Publishing Company. Originally appeared in *Vertex*.

Sharking Down, Brain Terminal, Copyright © 1974, 1975 by Mankind Publishing Company. Originally appeared in somewhat different form in *Vertex*.

Years Later, © 1976 by Edward Bryant.

In addition the author should like to thank Thames and Hudson, Ltd., for permission to quote from *Tao* by Philip Rawson and Laszlo Legeza, Copyright © 1973 by Thames and Hudson, Ltd., London.

Finally, grateful thanks are offered to the editors who nurtured this first volume of Cinnabar stories through birth: Gary Meadows, Ellen Couch, H. W. Griffin. Other profuse thanks go to the editors who liked these tales sufficiently to publish them individually in magazines and anthologies: Robert Hoskins, Robin Scott Wilson, Terry Carr, Don Pfeil. Thanks as well to Christine Cosgriffe Meyers who is responsible for the arrangement at the beginning of *Brain Terminal*. And acknowledgment also to Joan Bernott, who pioneered in the writing of Cinnabar stories.

Contents

"*Perhaps the most powerfully symbolic natural substance of all, which has a profound meaning, is cinnabar. This is a rosy-purple crystalline stone, sulphide of mercury. Ground up, it is the red pigment used in painting. But in Taoist symbolism and magic it represents the nuclear energy of joined yang and yin, which is to be fired in the internal crucible by alchemical yoga, to generate the yogi's immortality—just as mercury is produced from the rock by calcining it, when the sulphur releases a shining metallic fluid.*"

—PHILIP RAWSON and LASZLO LEGEZA
from *Tao*

Introduction:

Everyday Life in the City at the Center of Time

The title above seems infinitely more interesting than "Where *Do* You Get Your Ideas," which really is what this introduction is all about. Yet both titles, in the finest tradition of Cinnabar, reflect into each other like parallel mirrors lining a hallway. Well, almost. It may take a while to notice that the images in that procession marching to infinity do not duplicate themselves with complete fidelity.

However subtly, entropy does sneak in; and into the writer as well as the work. But that's another story. . . .

What I'm trying to work toward is the observation that Cinnabar is a city of infinite diversity, an opportunity for the exercise of endless alternatives. However superficially idealistic, that facet of the city demonstrates its Damoclean nature.

"May you live in interesting times." Remember, that's a Chinese *curse*.

That's essentially what I wish to tell you about Cinnabar itself. Need I indicate that City Center marks the focal point of all time? That the time stream cascades into Cinnabar in a multidimensional vortex? That the city lies only as distant from us as several freeway exits and uncountable parsecs and millennia? The particulars will unfold themselves.

Now the inhabitants of Cinnabar—*them* I want to mention: Tourmaline Hayes, the Network sex star; Jade Blue, hybrid catmother; the *Carcharodon megalodon* Sidhe; Harry Vincent Blake, the twentieth-century college boy who fell down the rabbit hole; Cougar Lou, the last hero; Leah Sand, melancholy media artist; Obregon, the never-quite-completely-mad scientist; and all the others. I hope you like meeting them.

Back up the line, where the key word was diversity, I meant to write something about story ideas. Let me hasten to say that Cinnabar is no mere fictional construct; it *exists* on one level or another. Which levels? Ambiguity is just another urban renewal project in Cinnabar.

These stories are visions of the city filtered through my mind and assembled into a partial mosaic. Any good mental puzzle should have its clues. Here are some of the subjective pieces:

(a) Back in the late nineteen-thirties and early forties, when my mother was a young woman living in Brooklyn, she spent her summers on a dude ranch in Peekskill, New York. The dude ranch was called the Cinnabar.

(b) Meanwhile, my father, having been reared in Colorado, had run away to sea and joined the Merchant Marine in 1932. From there he joined the United States Navy.

All of which leads to (c): the summer of 1940. My father was sitting around the Brooklyn Navy Yard with a buddy, both of them wondering how to spend a leave. My father closed his eyes and stabbed a pencil into a map of New York State. Right. Peekskill. The Cinnabar.

Five years passed. I was born precisely three weeks after the bombing of Hiroshima. Can anyone wonder that romance plays such an integral role in the everyday life of Cinnabar?

(d) I grew up in southern Wyoming, spending years both on ranches and in a small town. Like many readers-turned-writers of speculative fiction, I started reading SF for escape value. Seeking escape velocity, I looked for trajectories terminating somewhere outside a small, rural community.

(e) Cats. I can appreciate their proclivity for staring into apparently empty corners. Cats know and understand what lies beyond the mirror (which is where, of course, you'll find signposts to Cinnabar).

(f) In July 1969, at the Clarion Workshop in Science Fiction and Fantasy, visiting author Harlan Ellison gave us would-be writers an overnight assignment. As an exercise, we all were to create an entire page of narrative hooks, those catchy first lines of stories designed to snag the attention and interest of the average reader.

I thought my cleverest invention was: "One day the Pope forgot to take her Pill." That's a story I've never written and probably never will. On the other hand, one of my opening lines down near the bottom of the page was: "The road to Cinnabar was lined exclusively with the burned-out shells of school buses." That was the first time the city had cropped up in my prose.

(g) For many years I've read and admired the work of English writer J. G. Ballard, especially his stories of the perennially decadent community of Vermilion Sands.

(h) It's because of (g), I suspect, that I've been seduced into a peculiar affair with Venice, California—Vermilion Sands West.

(i) The epigraph came after the book. All but

one of the stories in this collection were finished before someone pointed out to me the Taoist significance of cinnabar. Naturally I was fascinated and excited.

* * *

Cinnabar, doomed city of hope, haven for paradoxes. I think the above are all the historical notes I want to include now. I'd like to finish up this introduction with just two wishes: first, that the reader find in this story collection a sum greater than the simple addition of the individual pieces; and second, that at one point or another, the reader will wish that he or she were in the city where these tales are set.

To paraphrase W. C. Fields very loosely, all things considered, I know I would rather be in Cinnabar.

EDWARD BRYANT

Denver
August 1974

1

The
Road
to
Cinnabar

It wove through the warp of the desert; a dusty trail looping around wind-eroded buttes, over dry stream beds, among clumps of gray scrub brush. Straighter, but always within sight of the roadway, was the elevated train track. No trains had run in centuries and the track was streaked with verdigris. Though there were seldom travelers to hear it, the wind in the trestles shrilled atonal scherzos.

Closer to the city, the road was lined with the burned-out shells of what had once been buses.

Then came the green belt, a mile-wide sward of grass and trees continually tended by small silent machines. Here walked occasional lovers, and others.

At last, the city. Cinnabar was a flux of glass towers and metal walls perched atop red cliffs crumbling down to a narrow band of beach and then to ocean.

The desert. The greenbelt. The city. The sea. There seemed very little more to the world. The elevated railroad was rumored to run to a place called Els. But no one was quite sure; no one remembered ever having traveled so far.

One day a man came into sight on the road to Cinnabar. He marched in from the desert toward the

city, whistling martial tunes as he walked. He was a
tall man, and thin. His sweat-stained white burnoose
flapped back in the wind like bat wings. His hood was
pulled far forward for shade but could not hide the
long hooknose. Upon reaching the greenbelt he stopped
to rest. Strolling lovers eyed him incuriously.

"I'm looking for an inn or hotel of some sort," he
called to one pair. The couple stopped and exchanged
glances. The girl, who was pale and beautiful except
for a jagged scar down her left cheek, laughed silently at some private amusement. Her companion looked
thoughtful.

"Try the Coronet," said the young man.

The traveler gestured impatiently. "I'm new to the
city. Direct me."

"Just follow the road."

"The sign of the crown," said the girl in a voice
so low it barely rose above the fountain's ripple.

"Grateful," said the traveler. He walked away toward the road.

"Stranger?"

He turned and the young man called, "How long
did it take you to cross the desert?"

The traveler opened his mouth to answer, then
closed it in confusion as he realized he had no answer. Both laughing now, the couple walked away. The
stranger shook his head and drank at one of the foun-
tains before continuing into Cinnabar.

The bubbles tickled her throat. Leah Sand put
down her glass of iced ginger ale and relaxed. She sat
in her customary chair in the front room of the Coronet. Across the planed-oak tabletop the afternoon sun
warmed carefully defined squares of hardwood.

"Care for an ice to go with the drink, Miss
Leah?" The voice cut through the dobro song on the
jukebox and the rhythmic, incoherent patterns of tour-
ist-talk. She looked up.

"What flavors?"

The innkeeper Matthias Kaufmann counted labo-
riously on his fingers: "Um, pineapple, chocolate,
watercress, just three."

"No lime?"

"No lime. Stock hasn't come in this week."

Leah flashed him a smile. "Thanks. I'll wait on it."

Enchanted as always by Leah's dark beauty, Kaufmann returned the smile over his shoulder as he walked ponderously away. Into the path of a serving girl. The collision didn't jar the innkeeper. But the girl was deflected toward a table of tourists who watched the approaching debacle with bovine expressions. Tourists, table and serving girl collapsed in a welter of cola drinks and watercress ices.

The serving girl began to wail, the drowned tourists mumbled and moved spastically like gaffed flounders, and Kaufmann was enraged. "Clumsy scullion! Retard!" The girl cried louder.

"Enrique!" said the innkeeper. "Gonzago!" Identically short and swarthy, the two men appeared from a back room. They were the bouncers, generally used only at night when a rougher trade frequented the Coronet.

"Discipline her!" Kaufmann pointed to the serving girl who was now choking on her sobs. "Perhaps she can learn some coordination."

Gonzago took the girl's wrists and dragged her to the center of the front room. Enrique produced a coil of rope and bound her hands together. Then he tossed the coil up and over one of the ceiling timbers. The two men hauled on the rope and soon the girl dangled, her toes centimeters above the floor.

Enrique grasped the back of the girl's high collar and pulled hard. The blouse ripped; the girl's back was golden in the light of imminent dusk. Gonzago handed Kaufmann a long black whip.

"This is for your stupid clumsiness," said the innkeeper, drawing back his arm.

"What's going on here?"

Kaufmann stopped in mid-motion, lowered his hand. In concert, everyone looked toward the door.

"Who the hell are you?" asked the innkeeper.

The gaunt man in the burnoose stepped into the Coronet. "Cafter. Wylie Cafter."

"Oh." Kaufmann turned back to his victim and again raised the whip.

"Don't do that." In three steps he was beside Kaufmann. Cafter's hand dipped and took the whip away from the innkeeper. Gonzago and Enrique moved in, menacingly, one on either side. For a dilated moment Kaufmann and the stranger stared at each other.

The innkeeper backed down. He murmured an obscenity and turned to Gonzago. "Okay, cut her down." Kaufmann walked back to his usual position behind the bar as the suspended serving girl swooned to the floor. She was immediately carried into the kitchen by two buxom cooks.

Gonzago and Enrique retreated to their back room. Outside the inn, the sun had touched the ocean.

"Tondelaya Beach is even more beautiful at dawn," said Leah. Cafter, standing close by her table, stared out the window.

"The length of the afternoon hardly justifies such a brief sunset," he said.

"It was a long afternoon for you?"

"Very. And dry."

"Then sit," said Leah. She motioned to a serving girl.

Cafter pulled a chair away from the table and sat. Leah was very beautiful, and he had nowhere else to go. "Dark beer," he ordered.

"What do you do?"

"I'm a labor organizer."

"Indeed? I'm fascinated." And Cafter knew that she was.

There was a pop of displaced air as an object the size and hue of a robin's egg appeared on the table. Leah picked it up, rapped it smartly on the oak and extracted a folded paper from among the pieces.

"It's probably from the Network." She unfolded the message, her lips moving silently as she read. "Yes." The note and the broken shell of the carrier evaporated into the air.

Leah pushed her chair back. "I'm sorry, Wylie. I've got to go. But I'll see you again."

Cafter hesitated. "Soon?"

"Soon for you. I have to go in toward the city's center."

"I'll miss you."

"Will you really?" Leah smiled, but her eyes were puzzled. "You're not supposed to."

Cafter sipped his beer and looked down at the table. "Agreed. Let's just say I wish you wouldn't go so that I could have time to know you better."

"Wylie, that's not what I—" Distracted, she set her glass down and rose from the table. Then, impulsively, she bent and kissed Cafter's forehead. "I'll see you." A flash of crinoline skirts and an on-the-way smile to Kaufmann, and she was gone.

"Hey, Lash," yelled Cafter to the innkeeper. "Give me another beer."

In this outskirt of Cinnabar, the night was presaged by an all-too-brief dusk. Measured out in empty bottles, the dark pressed against Cafter's window before he had finished the third beer. He took a final swallow and left the emptying Cornet. The street was deserted; Cafter walked a cracked and buckled sidewalk past a line of storefronts whose shades were drawn and doors locked. Around the first corner he found a small park with a raised, grassy center, a few benches, a stone obelisk of man-height, and a blank plaque. Cafter touched the metal. His fingers told him there once had been an inscription, now worn smooth. He tried to trace out the message, but it was too weathered. Only four numerals, more deeply carved, remained. 2 . . . 3 . . . They almost followed the whorls of his fingertips. 96 . . .

Cafter sat on a bench until the darkness was complete. He faced south, the direction of the desert road and the elevated tracks to Els. Near the horizon, the stars were like the eyes of desert animals fractionally trapped by firelight, cold and unblinking. Cafter tracked familiar patterns up the night sky to the zenith, where the stars twinkled in many colors. Standing, he turned toward the north, toward the distant center of Cinnabar. He saw the stars flash faster until the constellations merged in a white glow above the city's center.

Lights in the street switched on and the trees, grass and benches were very real again, and the dark sky receded. Cafter slowly walked back to the Coronet. More than thirty ground cycles were now parked outside the inn and Cafter had to thread his way carefully through a garden of steel.

The noise—he had to push through it like a second door as he entered the Coronet. The jukebox was turned up and it shored the human decibels with a deep heavy beat from Moog and percussion section.

Leah's table was vacant so Cafter sat there. He saw that all the tourists had gone. The front room was crowded with cyclers, giant muscular men with their giant muscular women. All were identically dressed in filthy trews, an Indian swastika with counterclockwise arms sewn as a patch on the back of each sleeveless jacket. All, male and female alike, were shaved hairless. The air smelled of beer farts, sweat and urine. The smaller tables had been shoved aside in the right half of the room and a pool table installed. Among the cyclers' rough patterns stalked the bouncers Enrique and Gonzago; not furtive, nor obtrusive, but with an air of readiness. Behind the bar Matthias Kaufmann poured beers in mechanical succession.

"Everything meshes so well," said Cafter quietly.

"Sir, may I help you?"

Cafter looked up at the girl. "Dark beer." All the serving girls had blue yes.

"Right away, sir." All the serving girls wore their long blonde hair in braids.

Balancing an empty tray, she moved off toward the bar. Did all the serving girls perform identically in bed? Cafter pleasantly pondered that.

He sat beer-sipping for an hour as the Coronet clockworked along. Then—the alien intrusion:

(1) A man nearly two and a half meters high, a head taller than any of the cyclers. He was heavily muscled in proportion and his skin was the blue-black of the sky before rain.

(2) A dwarf dressed in yellow and purple motley. He carried two silver cases, slung by leather straps so that one rested on either hip.

(3) A slim albino girl who carried a multilensed camera gleaming and faceted like a spider's eye. The trio entered the Coronet single file, gingerly protecting their equipment from lurching cyclers. No one seemed to notice them except Cafter.

The crew trekked through the sweaty bodies in an arc whose apogee was Cafter's table. Ignoring the seated man, the albino and the dwarf placed their gear in front of his glass.

"I'll get us a pitcher," said their leader. He started for the bar.

"Make it quick, Trillinor," said the swarf.

Cafter sat still, looking up at the albino girl and across at the dwarf, both of whom stood with their backs to him. Trillinor took a pitcher of beer from the bar in front of Kaufmann. The innkeeper didn't acknowledge the usurpation; he just picked up a clean pitcher from the towel behind him and placed it under the spout.

"That's a nice camera," said Cafter.

The girl and the dwarf slowly turned. The dwarf looked at Cafter, beside him, above him, behind him. "Did you hear it?"

"I think so, Reg." The girl's brow wrinkled delicately.

"I said that's a nice camera."

"I *did*!" said Reg.

"It sees it!" said the girl.

"Sees what?" Trillinor was back, his long fingers wrapped around a pitcher of dark beer.

"The camera!" said Reg. "It said it sees it. And Fiona heard it too."

The girl nodded.

"Of course I see the camera," said Cafter. "Do you think the bloody thing's invisible?"

The trio stared at him. Then Trillinor swiftly bent and grabbed Cafter by the collar, hauling him out of the chair. With the other hand the giant slapped

Cafter hard twice, then dropped him back into the chair. He swayed, putting his palms on the table for support.

"You, uh, still see the camera?" asked the dwarf.

"Yes, I—" Cafter had time to say. Trillinor sent him sprawling with another openhanded slap.

"No more," Fiona urged. "You'll damage it."

Cafter, half sitting up with the support of his elbows, had the sense to say nothing.

"We'd better report this to Leah," said Reg.

"Agreed," said Trillinor. "Get your gear."

The other two picked up the camera and the silver cases. Again in single file, the trio reached the door and exited. The girl Fiona glanced back at Cafter expressionlessly.

Cafter painfully got up and replaced his overturned chair. He wished there were something stiffer to drink; then gulped the remainder of his beer. Cafter tapped the empty glass on the table. Blood trickled to the end of his nose and began to drip on the table. It tickled slightly.

At the bar, Kaufmann struck a serving girl with his fist. Too hurried, she had dropped a full pitcher.

It was time.

"Do you *like* working for Kaufmann?" Cafter asked.

"Oh yes," said the serving girl. "Very much, sir."

"Even when he hits you?"

"Well—" She looked demurely at the planking. "After all, sir, he *is* the innkeeper."

"But wouldn't you like to stop working and become a tourist? You know, wear a knit shirt with an alligator totem over the heart? Sit around the Coronet all day and eat fruit ices?"

"Awwr . . . no sir." The half-witted busboy wagged his head vehemently. "Aah! No sir!"

"Well," said Cafter. "Well." He hesitated. "What would you like to be?"

The busboy looked at him doubtfully. "Anything?"

The organizer nodded.

The beatific smile drew Cafter's gaze away from the crazed eyes. "Oh sir, I wanna be a cycler."

Cafter smiled weakly. "We'll see."

"This drudgery needn't continue."

The first cook, arms akimbo, appraised Cafter. "Drudgery? God, I've gave the best years of my life here in this kitchen." She sighed, and Cafter couldn't help turning away from her foul breath. "I got to taste everything I spices," she said apologetically.

"How about you?" Cafter said, addressing the other cook. "Wouldn't you like to see working conditions improve?"

"Me? God, I've gave the best years of my life here in this kitchen."

"You're being exploited."

"Not me," said Enrique, smugness obtruding. "I got a good thing with the boss. Pay's not bad. 'Course it's a little dangerous once in a while . . ." He shrugged. "But hell, that's what I'm paid for."

"Me too," said Gonzago.

"You've been disturbing my employees," said Kaufmann.

"I've been encouraging group solidarity," said Cafter.

"Hasn't worked, huh?" The innkeeper stacked the clean glasses in a neat pyramid. His motions were quick and sure.

Cafter wanted to topple the pyramid of glasses. "No."

"Well, it won't."

"Any particular reason?"

Kaufmann placed a glass on the apex. "It's the natural order of things."

My heart isn't in this, meditated Cafter.

They found him in one of Cinnabar's many pocket parks. Cafter was bent over the verge of an old stone fountain, watching a sundial. Further out, three sprays hung a fine curtain in the afternoon. Closer, the sundial was a clear crystal disc with intaglio numerals. It was suspended over a half-meter maelstrom where the water was sucked away to be recirculated.

Cafter dropped a brown-veined leaf into the whirlpool and watched it rotate clockwise, slowly at first, then faster, until it finally whirled down the vortex in the center.

He felt a hand touch his shoulder and without looking, covered it with his own. "It was a very long night," he said.

"It was a longer month," said Leah.

He finally turned his head and looked beyond Leah to the little group standing in the crescent-shaped shadows of a kama tree: the giant Trillinor, the dwarf Reg and coral-eyed Fiona. "What have they to do with you?"

"They work with me," said the girl. "They are my recording crew."

"You know my next question."

"Historical documentaries, mostly. My speciality. I'm still a novice."

"You?"

"I direct." Her fingers traced a line along his jaw, almost a caress.

Cafter winced as she touched one of the bruises. "Your man Trillinor—he's none too gentle."

"He told me," Leah said. "When you evidenced seeing the crew, he knew your conditioning had broken. He thought he could jog you back into repair."

"Repair." Bitterness underlay the word. "You refer to me as a thing rather than a man."

Leah said nothing, continuing to stroke his face.

"When I walked out of the desert," said Cafter. "That's when I suspected my humanity. Two lovers asked about my crossing the desert. I knew then that I didn't know." His head dropped forward. "Reality is my deadliest enemy."

"As it is of us all," Leah murmured.

"But I still like you," said Cafter. "Whoever you are. Whatever." He paused. "I expect in me that's an aberration. Still, I don't suppose that . . ."

She said nothing.

"No, I suppose not." Cafter gazed into the fountain and saw a shadow lengthen over the rippling water. He closed his eyes as Trillinor gently touched a nerve center in the back of his neck.

The giant picked up Cafter's body and carefully cradled it. "Wonky simulacra," he said, head shaking slowly. Leah continued to face the stone fountain.

One day a man came into sight on the road to Cinnabar.

"Ready for retake," said Trillinor.

Leah sat at her usual table in the Coronet waiting for Kaufmann to bring an iced ginger ale. As always in Cinnabar, the day was warm. Yet Leah shivered. She waited for the player to arrive, and wondered if perhaps someone in Cinnabar were recording a documentary on directors.

2

Jade
Blue

"And this," said Timnath Obregon, "is the device I have invented to edit time."

The quartet of blurred and faded ladies from the Craterside Park Circle of Aesthetes made appreciative sounds; the whisper of a dry wind riffling the plates of a long-out-of-print art folio.

"Time itself."

"Fascinating, yes."

"Quite."

The fourth lady said nothing, but pursed wrinkled lips. She fixed the inventor in a coquettish gaze. Obregon averted his eyes. How, he wondered, did he deserve to be appreciated in this fashion? He had begun to wish the ladies would leave him to his laboratory.

"Dear Mr. Obregon," said the hitherto silent one. "You have no idea how much we appreciate the opportunity to visit your laboratory. This district of Cinnabar was growing tedious. It is so refreshing to encounter an eminent personality such as yourself."

Obregon's smile was strained. "I thank you, but my fame may be highly transitory."

Four faces were enraptured.

"My APE—" The inventor took a cue from the concert of rising eyebrows. "Ah, that's my none-too-clever acronym for the artificial probability enhancer. My device seems on the brink of being invented

12

simultaneously—or worse, first—by a competitor at the Tancarae Institute. One Dr. Sebastian Le Goff."

"Then this machine is not yet, um, fully invented?"

"Not fully developed. No, I'm afraid not." Obregon thought he heard one of the ladies *tsking,* an action he had previously believed only a literary invention. "But it's very, very close to completion," he hastened to say. "Here, let me show you. I can't offer a full demonstration, of course, but—" He smiled winningly.

Obregon seated himself before the floor-to-ceiling crystal pillar which was the APE. He placed his hands on a brushed-metal console. "These are the controls. The keyboard is for the programing of probability changes." He stabbed the panel with an index finger; the crystal pillar glowed fluorescent orange. "The device is powered inductively by the vortical time streams which converge in the center of Cinnabar." His finger darted again and the pillar resumed its transparency. "For now I'm afraid that's all I can show you."

"Very pretty, though."

"I think blue would be so much more attractive."

"I found the most cunning sapphire curtain material yesterday."

"Tea would be marvelous, Mr. Obregon."

"Please, ladies. Call me Timnath." The inventor walked to a tangle of plastic tubing on an antiseptic counter. "I'm an habitual tea drinker, so I installed this instant brewing apparatus." He slid a white panel aside and removed five delicate double-handled cups. "The blend for today is black dragon pekoe. Satisfactory with everyone?"

Nodding of heads; brittle rustle of dying leaves.

"Cream and sugar?"

The tall one: "Goat cream, please."

The short one: "Two sugars, please."

The most indistinct one: "Nothing, thank you."

The flirtatious one: "Mother's milk, if you would."

Obregon punched out the correct combinations on the teamaker's panel and rotated the cups under the spigot.

From behind him one of the ladies said, "Timnath, what will you do with your machine?"

Obregon hesitated. "I'm not sure, really. I've always rather liked the way things are. But I've invented a way of changing them. Maybe it's a matter of curiousity."

Then he turned and distributed the tea. They sat and sipped and talked of science and the arts.

"I firmly believe," said the inventor, "that science *is* an art."

"Yes," said the flirtatious lady. "I gather that you pay little attention to either the practical or commercial applications of technology." She smiled at him from behind steepled fingers.

"Quite so. Many at the Institute call me a dilettante."

The tall lady said, "I believe it's time to go. Timnath, we thank you for allowing us to impose. It has been a pleasure." She dashed her teacup to the tile floor. Her companions followed suit.

Startled by their abruptness, Obregon almost forgot to smash his own nearly empty cup. He stood politely as the ladies filed past him to the door. Their postures were strangely alike; each in her brown dress reminded him of the resurrectronic cassowaries he admired at the Natural History Club.

"A pleasure," repeated the tall lady.

"Quite." (The short one.)

Exit the flirt. "Perhaps I'll be seeing you again soon?" Her gaze lingered and Obregon looked aside, mumbling some pleasantry.

The fourth lady, the one whose features had not seemed to jell, paused in the doorway. She folded her arms so that the hands tucked into her armpits. She jumped up and down, flapping her truncated limbs. "Scraw! Scraw!" The soft door whuffed shut.

Taken aback, Obregon felt the need for another cup of tea and he sat down. On the table a small black cylinder stood on end. It could have been a tube of lip-salve. Apparently it had been forgotten by one of his guests. Curious, he picked it up. It was very light. He unscrewed one end; the cylinder was empty. Obregon raised the object to his nose. There was the distinct acrid tang of silver iodide emulsion.

"It appears," said Obregon softly, "to be an empty film cannister."

A child's scream in a child's night. A purring, enfolding comfort. A loneliness of nightmares and the waking world and the indistinct borderland. A feline reassurance.

"Don't cry, baby. I'll hold you close and rock you."

George buried his face in the soft blue fur which blotted his tears. "Jade Blue, I love you."

"I know," said the catmother softly. "I love you too. Now sleep."

"I can't," George said. "They'll find me again." His voice rose in pitch and his body moved restlessly; he clutched at Jade Blue's warm flank. "They'll get me in the shadows, and some will hold me down, and the one will reach for—"

"Dreams," said Jade Blue. "They can't hurt you." Feeling inside her the lie. Her fingerpads caressed the boy's head and drew it close again.

"I'm afraid." George's voice was distantly hysterical.

The governess guided the boy's head. "Drink now." His lips found the rough nipple and sucked instinctively. Her milk soothed, gently narcotic, and he swallowed slowly. "Jade Blue," the whisper was nearly inaudible. "I love you." The boy's body began to relax.

Jade Blue rocked him slowly, carefully wiping away the thin trickle of milk from one corner of his mouth, then lay down and cuddled the boy against her. After a time she also slept.

And awoke, night-wary. She was alone. With an angry snarl, quickly clipped off, she struggled from the bed. Jade Blue extended all her senses and caught a subtle scent of fear, a soft rub of something limp on flagstones, the quick flash of shadow on shadow.

A black, vaguely anthropomorphic shape moved in the darkness of the doorway. There were words, but

they were so soft as to seem exhaled rather than spoken: "Forget it, pussy." A mouth gaped and grinned.
"He's ours, cat."

Jade Blue screamed and leaped with claws out-
thrust. The shadow figure did not move; it squeaked
and giggled as the catmother tore it apart. Great portions of shadowstuff, light as ash, flew about the room.
The mocking laughter faded.

She paused in the doorway, flanks heaving, sucking in breath. Her wide, pupilless eyes strained to in-
terpret the available light. Sharp-pointed ears tilted
forward. The enormous house, very quiet; except—

Jade Blue padded swiftly down the hall, easily
threading the irregular masses of inert sculpture. She
ran silently, but in her mind:

Stupid cat! That shadow was a decoy, a diversion.
  Foolish woman! The boy is my trust.
Find him. If anything has happened to him, I will
     be punished.
  If anything has happened to him, I shall kill
     myself.
A sound. The game room.
  They couldn't have taken him far.
That bitch Merreile! I could tear out her throat.
  How could she do it to him?
Close now. Quietly.

The double doors of the game room stood ajar.
Jade Blue slipped between their baroquely carved
edges. The room was large and echoing with the para-
phernalia of childhood: glaze-eyed hobbyhorses, infinite shelves of half-assembled model kits, ranks of
books and tapes and dot-cases, balls, mallets, frayed
creatures spilling stuffing, instruments of torture, gaming
boards, and an infrared spectrometer. The catmother
moved carefully through George's labyrinth of memories.

In a cleared space in the far end she found him.
George lay on his back, spread-eagled, straining weakly against intangible fetters. Around him flocked the

moving shadows, dark succubus-shapes. One of them crouched low over the boy and brushed shadow lips around flesh.

George's mouth moved and he mewed weakly, like a kitten. He raised his head and stared past the shadows at Jade Blue.

The catmother resisted her first berserker reaction. Instead she stepped quickly to the near wall and found the lighting panel. She pressed a square, and dim illumination glowed from the walls; pressed harder and the light brightened, then seared. Proper shadows vanished. The moving shadow creatures raveled like poorly woven fabric and were gone. Jade Blue felt an ache beginning in her retinas and dimmed the light to a bearable level.

On the floor George was semiconscious. Jade Blue picked him up easily. His eyes were open, their movements rapid and random, but he was seeing nothing. Jade Blue cradled the boy close and walked down the long hallways to their bedroom.

George was dreamless the remainder of the long night. Once, closer to wakening, he stirred and lightly touched Jade Blue's breasts. "Kitty, kitty," he said. "Nice kitty." Friendlier shadows closed about them both until morning.

When George awoke he felt a coarse grade of sand abrade the inside of his eyelids. He rubbed with his fists, but the sensation lingered. His mouth was dry. George experimentally licked the roof of his mouth; it felt like textured plastic. There was no taste. He stretched, winced, joints aching. The syndrome was familiar; it was the residue of bad dreams.

"I'm hungry." He reclined against crumpled blue satin. A seed of querulousness, "I'm hungry." Still no response. "Jade Blue?" He was hungry, and a bit lonely. The two conditions were complementary in George, and both omnipresent.

George swung his legs off the bed. "Cold!" He drew on the pair of plush slippers; then, otherwise naked, he walked into the hall.

Sculptures in various stages of awakening nodded at George as he passed. The sylization of David yawned and scratched its crotch. " 'Morning, George."

"Good morning, David."

The replica of a Third Cycle odalisque ignored him as usual.

"Bitch," George mumbled.

"Mommy's boy," mocked the statue of Victory Rampant.

George ignored her and hurried past.

The abstract Pranksters Group tried to cheer him up, but failed miserably.

"Just shut up," said George. "All of you."

Eventually the sculptures were left behind and George walked down a paneled hallway.

The hall finally described a klein turn, twisted in upon itself, and exited into the laboratory of Timnath Obregon.

Luminous pearl walls funneled him toward the half-open door. George saw a quick swirl of lab smock. He was suddenly conscious of the silence of his steps. He knew he should announce himself. But then he overheard the dialogue:

"If his parents would come home, that might help." The voice was husky, the vowels drawn out. Jade Blue.

"Not a chance," said Obregon's tenor. "They're too close to City Center by now. I couldn't even begin to count the subjective years before they'll be back."

George waited outside the doorway and listened.

Jade Blue's voice complained. "Well, couldn't they have found a better time for a second honeymoon? Or third, or fourth, or whatever."

A verbal shrug. "They are, after all, researchers with a curious bent. And the wonders which lie closer to the center of Cinnabar are legendary. I can't blame them for their excursion. They *had* lived in this family group a rather long time."

"Oh shit, you idiot human! You're rationalizing."

"Not entirely. George's mother and father are sentients. They have a right to their own life."

"They also have responsibilities." Pause. "Merreile. That fathersucking little—"

"They couldn't have known when they hired her, Jade Blue. Her, um, peculiarities didn't become apparent until she had been George's governess for several months. Even then, no one knew the ultimate results."

"No one knew! No one cared, you mean."

"That's a bit harsh, Jade—"

"Listen, you pale imitation of an open mind. Can't you see? They're the most selfish people alive. They want to take nothing from themselves, give nothing to their son."

Silence for a few seconds.

Jade Blue again: "You're a kind man, but so damned obtuse!"

"I'm quite fond of George," said the inventor.

"And I also. I love him as one of my own. It's too bad his own parents don't."

In the hallway George was caught in an ambivalence of emotion. He missed his parents horribly. But he also loved Jade Blue. So he began to cry.

Obregon tinkered with a worms' warren of platinum filaments.

Jade Blue paced the interior of the laboratory and wished she could switch her vestigial tail.

George finished his milk and licked the last cookie crumb from his palm.

A large raven flapped lazily through a window in the far end of the lab. "Scraw! Scraw!"

"Ha!" The inventor snapped his fingers and glistening panes slid into place; the doors shut; the room was sealed. Apparently confused, the raven fluttered in a tight circle, screaming in hoarse echoes.

"Jade, get the boy down!" Obregon reached under the APE's console and came up with a cocked and loaded crossbow. The bird saw the weapon, snaprolled into a turn and dive, darted for the closest window. It struck the pane and rebounded.

George let Jade Blue pull him down under one of the lab tables.

Wings beat furiously as the raven caromed off a

wall, attempting evasive action. Obregon coolly aimed the crossbow and squeezed the trigger. The short square-headed quarrel passed completely through the raven and embedded itself in the ceiling. The bird, wings frozen in mid-flap, cartwheeled through the air and struck the floor at Obregon's feet. Stray black feathers autumnleafed to the floor.

The inventor gingerly toed the body; no movement. "Fool. Such underestimation." He turned to Jade Blue and his nephew, who were extracting themselves from beneath the table. "Perhaps I'm less distracted than you charge."

The catmother licked delicately at her rumpled blue fur. "Care to explain all this?"

Obregon picked up the body of the raven with the air of a man lifting a package of particularly fulsome garbage. "Simulacrum," he said. "A construct. If I dissected it properly I'd discover a quite sophisticated surveillance and recording system." He caught Jade Blue's unblinking green eyes. "It's a spy, you see." He dropped the carcass into the disposer, where it vanished in a golden flare and the transitory odor of well-done meat.

"It was big," said George.

"Good observation. Wingspread of at least two meters. That's larger than any natural raven."

"Who," asked Jade Blue, "is spying?"

"A competitor, fellow named Le Goff, a man of no certain ethics and fewer scruples. A day ago he brought his spies here to check the progress of my new invention. It was all done very clumsily so that I'd notice. Le Goff is worse than a mere thief. He mocks me." Obregon gestured toward the artificial probability enhancer.

"It's *that* he wishes to complete before I do."

"A crystal pillar?" said Jade Blue. "How marvelous."

"Quiet, cat. My machine can edit time. I will be able to alter the present by modifying the past."

"Is that all it does?"

Obregon seemed disgusted. "In my own home I don't need mockery."

"Sorry. You sounded pompous."

The inventor forced a laugh. "I suppose so. It's Le Goff who has driven me to that. All I've ever wanted was to be left in peace to work my theories. Now I feel I'm being forced into some sort of confrontation."

"And competition?"

Obregon nodded. "Just why, I don't know. I worked with Le Goff for years at the Institute. He was always a man of obscure motives."

"You're a good shot," said George.

Obregon self-consciously set the crossbow on the console. "It's a hobby. I'd only practiced with stationary targets before."

"Can I try it?"

"I think you're probably too small. It takes a great deal of strength to cock the bow."

"I'm not too small to pull the trigger."

"No," said Obregon. "You're not." He smiled. "After lunch we'll go out to the range. I'll let you shoot."

"Can I shoot a bird?"

"No, not a live one. I'll have some simulacrae made up."

"Timnath," said Jade Blue. "I don't suppose— No, probably not."

"What."

"Your machine. It can't change dreams."

Mother, Father, help me I don't want the dreams any more. Just the warm black that's all. Mother? Father? Why did you go when will you come back? You leave me left me make me hurt.

Uncle Timnath, get them bring them back. Tell them I hurt I need. Make them love me.

Jade Blue, rock me hold me love me bring them back now. No no don't touch me there you're like Merreile I don't want more bad dreams don't hurt don't—

And Merreile would come into his bedroom each evening to take him from his toys and prepare him for bed. She would undress him slowly and slip the nightshirt over his head, then sit cross-legged at the foot of the bed while he lay back against the pillow.

"A story before sleeping? Of course, my love. Shall I tell again of the vampires?

"Do you remember my last telling, love? No? Perhaps I caused you to forget." And she would smile, showing the bands of scarlet cartilage where most people had teeth.

"Once upon a time, there was a little boy, much like you, who lived in an enormous old house. He was alone there, except for his parents and his loving governess.

"Oh, quite true that there were vampires hiding in the attic, but they weren't much like living creatures at all. They seldom ventured from the attic and the boy was never allowed to go there. His parents had forbidden him, despite the fact that the attic was filled with all manner of interesting and enjoyable things.

"The boy's curiosity grew and grew until one night he slipped out of his room and quietly climbed the stairs to the attic. At the top of the flight he paused, remembering his parents' warning. Then he recalled what he had heard about the strange treasures that lay within. He knew that warnings come from dull people and should be ignored. That barriers are made to be crossed. And then he opened the attic dor.

"Inside were rows of tables stacked high with every sort of game and toy imaginable. Between were smaller tables laden with candy and cakes and pitchers of delicious drink. The boy was never happier.

"At that moment the vampires came out to play. They looked much like you and me, except that they were black and very quiet and just as thin as shadows.

"They crowded around the boy and whispered to him to come join their games.

They loved the boy very much, because people came so seldom to the attic to visit. They were very honest (for folk so thin cannot hold lies) and the boy knew how silly his parents' warnings had been. Then they went off to the magic lands in the far end of the attic and played for hours and hours.

"What games, darling? I will show you."

And then Merreile would switch off the light and reach for him.

No, it can't change dreams, Timnath had said, musing. Then, looking through the catmother's eyes as though jade were glass, he said, *Give me time; I must think on it.*

They sat and talked in the blue bedroom.

"Did you ever have children like me?" George hugged his drawn-up knees.

"Not like you."

"I mean, were they kittens, or more like babies?"

"Both if you like. Neither." Her voice was neutral.

"You're not playing fair. Answer me." The child's voice was ancient, petulant from long practice.

"What do you want to know?"

George's fists beat a rapid tattoo on his knees. "Your children, what were they like? I want to know what happened to them."

Silence for a while. Small wrinkles under Jade Blue's lip, as though she held something bitter in her mouth. "They were never like anything."

"I don't understand."

"Because they *weren't*. They came from Terminex the computer. They lived in him and died in him; he placed the bright images in my brain."

George sat straighter; this was better than a bedtime story. "But why?"

"I'm the perfect governess. My maternal instincts are augmented. I've hostages in my mind." Each word was perfectly cut with gemstone edges.

Petulance softened to a child's compassion. "It makes you very sad."

"Sometimes."

"When I'm sad I cry."

"I don't," said Jade Blue. "I can't cry."

"I'll be your son," said George.

The hall of diurnal statues was still. Jade Blue prowled the shadows, seeking the slight sounds and odors and temperature differentials. The encroaching minutes frustrated and made her frantic. The many nights of sleepless watch—and the eventual betrayal by her body. Again she looked for a lost child.

Not in the game room this time; the hobbyhorses grinned vacantly.

Nor in the twenty gray parlors where George's ancestors kept an embalmed and silent vigil from their wall niches.

Nor in the attic, dusty and spiderwebbed.

Not in the dining hall, arboretum, kitchens, aquatorium, library, observatory, family rooms, or linen closets.

Not—Jade Blue ran down the oak hallway and the minute signs vindicated her caprice. She ran faster and when she hurled herself into the corner which kleined into the approach to Timnath Obregon's laboratory, her stomach turned queasily.

The door slid open at a touch. The lab was dimly illuminated by the distorted yellow lights of Cinnabar. Several things occurred at once:

—In front of her, a startled figure looked up from the console of Obregon's APE. A reeled measuring tape dropped and clattered on tile.

—Across the lab a group of capering shadow figures stopped the act they were committing on George's prone body and looked toward the door.

—A screeching bird-shape flapped down from the dark ceiling and struck at Jade Blue's eyes.

The catmother ducked and felt claws cut harmless runnels through fur. She rolled onto her back and lashed out, her own claws extended. She snagged something heavy that screamed and buffeted her face with feathered wings. She knew she could kill it.

Until the booted foot came down on her throat and Jade Blue looked up past the still-struggling bird-thing at whoever had been examining Obregon's invention. "Sorry," said the man, and pressed harder.

"George!" Her voice was shrill, strangled. "Help." And then the boot was too heavy to let by any words at all. The darkness thickened intolerably.

The pressure stopped. Jade Blue could not see, but —painfully—she could again breathe. She could hear, but she didn't know what the noises were. There were bright lights and Timnath's concerned face, and arms lifting her from the floor. There was warm tea and honey poured into a saucer. George was hugging her and his tears put salt in the tea.

Jade Blue rubbed her throat gingerly and sat up; she realized she was on a white lab table. On the floor a little way from the table was an ugly mixture of feathers and wet red flesh. Something almost unrecognizable as a man took a ragged breath.

"Sebastian," said Timnath, kneeling beside the body. "My dear friend." He was crying.

"Scraw!" said the dying man; and died.

"Did you kill him?" said Jade Blue, her voice hoarse.

"No, the shadows did."

"How?"

"Unpleasantly." Timnath snapped his fingers twice and the glittering labrats scuttled out from the walls to clean up the mess.

"Are you all right?" George stood very close to his governess. He was shivering. "I tried to help you."

"I think you did help me. We're all alive."

"He did, and we are," said Timnath. "For once, George's creations were an aid rather than a hindrance."

"I still want you to do something with your machine," said Jade Blue.

Timnath looked sadly down at the body of Sebastian Le Goff. "We have time."

Time progressed helically, and one day Timnath pronounced his invention ready. He called George and Jade Blue to the laboratory. "Ready?" he said, pressing the button which would turn on the machine.

"I don't know," said George, half hiding behind Jade Blue. "I'm not sure what's happening."

"It will help him," said Jade Blue. "Do it."

"He may be lost to you," said Timnath.

George whimpered. "No."

"I love him enough," said the governess. "Do it."

The crystal pillar glowed bright orange. A fine hum cycled up beyond the auditory range. Timnath tapped on the keyboard: GEORGE'S DREAMS OF THE SHADOW VAMPIRES ARE AS NEVER WERE. MERREILE NEVER EXISTED. GEORGE IS OPTIMALLY HAPPY.

The inventor paused, then stabbed a special button: REVISE.

The crystal pillar glowed bright orange. A fine hum cycled up beyond the auditory range. Timnath tapped on the keyboard: GEORGE'S DREAMS OF THE SHADOW VAMPIRES ARE AS NEVER WERE. MERREILE NEVER EXISTED. GEORGE IS REASONABLY HAPPY.

Timnath considered then pushed another button: ACTIVATE. "That's it," he said.

"Something's leaving us," Jade Blue whispered.

They heard a scuff of footsteps in the outer hall. Two people walking. There was the clearing of a throat, a parental cough.

"Who's there?" said Jade Blue, knowing.

3

Gray Matters

The city. Forever the city. Within it rots the tissue of dreams.

Tourmaline Hayes—"the bright and sensual, sometimes cynical Tourmaline Hayes" according to *The Guide to the Stars*—muses along the thin border between sleep and wakefulness. By choice she lies alone.

She allows the characters to press their noses against her interface with fantasy. The most affecting face is that of Francie, enduring ingenue.

Tourmaline and Francie face each other across a gray, damp beach. Francie approaches with slow, deliberate steps. Tourmaline opens her arms in welcome.

She looks at Francie's face. Through the openings where Francie's eyes should be, she can see the night sky. Tourmaline stares, strains, searches the constellations for *Speculum,* the mirror.

It's a party like all other parties, and by any other name a *Walpurgisnacht.* Yet dull. So much sin, too often, breeds ennui. Everybody knows that. Everyone . . .

"—who is anybody," says Francie, completing an unconscious syllogism. She smiles up at Sternig, the critic of gay drama. She slightly sucks in her cheeks, hoping to emphasize the high cheekbones everyone says will be beautiful later in life when the skin of her face begins to tauten. It's a harmless deceit.

The gesture doesn't benefit Sternig. Two affinity

27

groups beyond them lounges Francie's prospective lover. Kandelman bestows largess upon three literary sycophants, who giggle shrilly. He leans back against a walnut bookcase, thumbs hooked in his belt, hips cantilevered forward. Kandelman's neglected his codpiece. It looks as though he's storing tennis balls behind the buttoned fly.

"Peanuts," says Sternig.

Francie's chin jerks up. "What?"

"Or pretzels. Whatever. You know, troll food." Sternig shrugs.

"I thought you said—"

"Party food progressively deteriorates," he says. "The second law of gastrodynamics."

Francie's little catamount tongue strokes nervously between lips.

"I need a drink," says Sternig. Apparently disinterested, "You want?"

"No." She smiles mechanically. "You'll excuse me? I have to use my spray."

He watches the back of her head blur in the aphrodisiac haze. Her diminishing skull takes all too long to vanish. Sternig brushes long brown hair back from his eyes. He mumbles his self-pity and yearns for beer, dark and draft.

The bathroom is decorated in a style the catalogue calls modern erotic. Surfaces gleam cold, opaque and hard. Francie's face explodes back at her from prismed mirrors. In her peripheral vision the white-on-white tiles fade to Arctic vagueness.

She takes the tube from her purse and hikes her skirt. The hiss echoes softly. Francie relaxes and enjoys a brief labial coolness. Scented excitement, no longer bland, she adjusts her panties. No hunter ever more carefully lubricated the action of her weapon.

Francie examines her reflection in the faceted medicine chest. Why is the flesh around her eyes so puffy? Her dark eyes had once snapped—a former lover told her that one passionate afternoon in a motel room in Tondelaya Beach. Francie's heart-shaped face creases in a frown. Her eyes have the puckered sheen of day-old ripe olives.

The door bangs open and shut; a ghost has passed.

"Got a spare douche?" says the newcomer.

"Need what I've got, Marlene."

Marlene removes a hairbrush from her purse. "Do you ever. Give me a shot."

"For Tourmaline?" She lazily proffers the jeweled tube. "Love to."

Marlene giggles and bares feral teeth. "Jealous, Francie? I wasn't."

Francie snaps shut the purse, barely missing Marlene's fingertips. "Shut up!"

"You're very sensitive, darling. Are *they* still sensitive?"

Francie says again, "Shut up."

The brush hisses through Marlene's light lank hair. The strokes are cadenced with her words. "I don't care, honey. Just because most guys have milk fetishes . . . I hope it's worth it."

"It will be."

"Kandelman's big on nipples." Marlene is laughing. She drops the hairbrush and it clatters across the tile counter. "*Extremely* big."

"Too big for you?"

"Hardly," says Marlene. "He's such a complete bastard."

Francie smiles. "I can take it." She stands up.

"Want to hear a riddle?" says Marlene maliciously. "What's eight inches long and glows in the dark?"

"Glows?"

"Sorry," says Marlene. "I meant 'grows.' "

Francie looks back from the doorway. "I love it."

Sternig is talking with Tourmaline Hayes, the sex star. Half a head taller, she slouches against the piano to make him feel at ease. Sternig smiles, aware of her charity.

"I caught all your last performances."

"Not exactly your sort of thing, I'd think."

"Don't confuse the work with the man," says Sternig.

Tourmaline's eyes are matched to her name. Their corners crinkle slightly as she smiles. Sternig smiles in return, relaxing. "I know, Sternig. You love everyone, but mainly women. Do you love me?"

Smiling. "Of course."

Laughing. "Liar. You love one person. Only one."

He stiffens. "Tourmaline—"

"Apart from yourself, of course."

"Tourmaline, don't—"

"It's not as though I hate her," says Tourmaline.

"Let's talk about you," says Sternig.

"You never learn, do you?"

"I'm only trying—"

"—to divert the conversation," finishes Tourmaline. "Do you know how many times we've gone through this?"

"Christ," says Sternig. "I don't want to talk about it. I don't want to think about it."

Tourmaline touches his cheek, silk to sandpaper. "The one's easy enough."

He lightly kisses her fingertips. "I'm beginning to forget the other."

"Doubly a liar." She snatches away her hand. "Sternig, Sternig, you stupid ass."

"I need another drink," Sternig says quickly. "Do you?"

"I'm not finished," she says, sloshing the glass. "And I'm not done with you either."

"Why me?" he asks.

"You're my good deed for the millennium." She tosses back her—for this evening—long green hair. "I can't save you from yourself, but maybe I can keep—" The rest is blotted by laughter. The life of the party has arrived.

"So that's exactly what I said. The bastard couldn't believe it." Secondary chuckles run through the party people. It's Jack Burton, star of the popular series "Jack Burton—Immortal." His show has just been renewed for its one-thousandth season and this party is the celebration.

Tourmaline smiles and speaks softly, as though reporting a sporting event: "Jack Burton grins at his friends, pumps hands, kisses lips, but there's a forced quality to the gaiety. He moves across the room well attended, but the congratulations verge on the perfunctory. His eyes—and how I envy that piercing blue —sparkle with intelligence, but I see the vagueness flicker now and again. Jack Burdon is like a ripe red tomato and inside him are worms."

"What?" says Sternig.

"Worms. They've begun eating through to his eyes."

Sternig grimaces. "You're morbid."

"Watch his eyes, Sternig. You'll see. Suddenly nothing there but blank holes."

"That drink," says Sternig. "I'm going to get it. Stay here. I'll bring two."

When he returns, Tourmaline Hayes still leans with her head against the piano. She accepts her new drink silently.

Sternig sips thoughtfully. "After the party—"

She looks at him. He cannot decipher her expression.

"After the party, I want you to go home with me."

Tourmaline smiles, more to herself than to Sternig. "I'm sorry, I can't."

Sternig would like to ask why not, but—

"Maybe another time," she says. "We're not ready for that. I'm going home with Marlene."

"I—"

She overrides him. "And your Francie will go home with Kandelman. And Jack Burton will go home with his agent. Sternig, who will take you home? Who?"

Instantly alone and lonely, Sternig would like to cry. But he can't. He's a big boy now. Has been for longer than he cares to remember. Longer than he can remember.

"Who?" Tourmaline repeats.

Sternig has to dream it, because the memory is too ancient and scoured to recall in his consciousness:

They determined to live happily ever after. Through a friend, Francie obtained the lease on a beach cottage on an isolated stretch of the coast. Sternig moved in his things from the cramped city apartment. The first few evenings they spent on the open porch watching the ocean, listening, feeling the last tailings of spray. They observed the rhythm of the waves sucking at the beach sand in millimeter portions. The house was set a hundred meters back from the water. They wouldn't have to worry for a long time.

Days, they swam in the early-morning sunshine before breakfast. Mornings were for work. Several times each week, Sternig flew the windhover into the city to see to the disposition of his column. Francie spent her mornings writing poetry and scanning tapes of her latest obsession, political history. She wrote essays which Sternig told her would be well received, had she ever bothered to submit them somewhere.

The air was heavy and sweet in the afternoon. The previous tenant had cultivated an extensive flower garden in back of the cottage. Lush beds sprawled among grassy blocks in a patchwork effect. Nothing exotic: scarlet tiger lilies, purple iris, brilliant yellow daisies. Flowers that bloomed repeatedly with a minimum of care.

Francie and Sternig made love in the grass. They lay quietly and smelled their own scent mingle with the heavy floral aroma.

"I want this to go on forever," said Francie. She looked up at her lover. "Can't it?"

"Yes," said Sternig, not then understanding the deceit of time.

Like all Sternig's dreams, it fades with awakening, leaving no specific words or images; only feelings.

Kandelman admires her breasts. He would touch them already, but etiquette demands a delay. Still, fifty percent of his eye contact is below her collar bone. Under his gaze, erectile tissue stiffens and her nipples poke against soft fabric. She loves it.

"What are you writing now?" Francie asks.

"I'm well into the new novel," says Kandelman. "It's a psychosexual thing."

"That's very interesting." Francie angles her chin, knowing her cheekbones appear to advantage. "What's it about?"

"Brothers and sisters. That's about all I can tell you at this point. The book's writing itself. I've got very little to do with the process, aside from feeding in the paper."

"Have you picked a title?"

"*Brothers and Sisters,* I think."

"Oh." Francie is losing interest in the novel. Unless, of course, Kandelman should volunteer a précis of a titillating passage.

"It's not really erotica," he says, "though it might sound like it from the title."

"Oh," she says vaguely. "I thought it might be, from the title."

"It may turn out that way," he hastens to say. "But for now it's a very serious book."

She says seriously, "Erotica *can* be serious."

He stares at her chest. Francie's breasts have assumed an orogenic significance in his mind. They are large, yet possess no hint of sag. They project without visible support. Kandelman wonders silently that he has not noticed them before this party.

"I think it can," Francie continues.

"What?" Kandelman breaks free of his preoccupation. "Oh yes. Of course it can."

"I'd like to see you write a really erotic book."

"Well," says Kandelman.

"I'd like to help you with it."

Kandelman realizes he could have predicted the entire sequence of conversation and is glad that he didn't.

The party is so brittle, thinks Sternig, at any moment it will shatter like hard candy. The great marble hall is festooned with streamers of candy-stripe crepe. Lighter-than-air balloons, fashioned in the image of extinct beasts, float from tethers. Sternig sips his drink in the shadow of a hippogriff.

With displeasure he stares across the swirling mass of the party at Francie and Kandelman, animatedly talking. They sit close together on a low foam couch, beneath the spread-antlered shelter of an inflated elk.

"Bitch," says Sternig.

"Who?" says Tourmaline. "Kandelman or your Francie?"

"Stop it." Sternig frowns. "She's not mine."

"Wasn't she?"

When did she go home with me? Sternig wonders. There was a time . . . Jack Burton was celebrating one of his renewals. She didn't go home with me, but we went to the beach from the party. Together . . .

> They drove out of the city on the Klein Expressway. He drove Francie's car, a low and powerful convertible. At speed he drifted it around the tight curves of each cloverleaf as the expressway redoubled upon itself. Francie cuddled against him, laughing, whispering in his ear. They exited at Tondelaya Beach, and between the towering red bluffs and the flat sea found a motel.
>
> Light, reflecting from the water, rippled across the ceiling. He gently lowered her to the bed and began to undo her hooks and eyes and buttons. She smiled up at him and he told Francie how her dark eyes were snapping with excitement.
>
> Soon, as he lay beside her, his own excitement became too great and he turned away, uncertain and apologetic.
>
> "No," she said. "Don't go soft on me."
>
> But—"I'm sorry." He could repeat that, but there was little else to say.

*What she said then was too cruel for
remembering.*

"I remember once," says Sternig. "When . . .
when . . ."

"Yes?" Tourmaline prompts.

"I can't remember," he says finally. "And I need
another drink."

"Can't remember? Or won't?"

"Can't," he says. "I think it's can't. I'm not really
sure. I have my mind sponged periodically. Don't
you?"

Tourmaline nods. "Occasionally. As seldom as I
can. I prefer to keep as many memories as possible.
Otherwise I tend to repeat my mistakes."

"In time," says Sternig, "we all repeat."

"Some of us more often than others." She gestures
across the hall. "Francie goes to the sponge once a
year, maybe more. I suspect her of monthly visits, even
weekly."

"I suppose she doesn't like her memories," he
says.

"She overdoes the forgetting. Her mind is always
fresh for the next party. All washed, whirled, fluffed,
tumbled, and spun dry. It could make me sad."

"It doesn't."

"No," Tourmaline says.

"You shouldn't hate her—" Sternig starts to say.

"Shut up," but her voice is still soft. "I know.
Now get yourself that drink."

*Periodically, but never so often as to
compromise the privacy of the place, Tourmaline came to visit at the beach cottage.
More than almost anything else, she loved to
swim naked in the sea. Late in the afternoon,
she lay with Francie on the swimming platform while Sternig fixed supper on the shore.
She massaged the taut muscles of Francie's
neck with strong, gentle fingers.*

"Tell me why you're upset."

Francie denied it.

"No," Tourmaline said. "I've known you too long and too well."

Francie was silent for a while, allowing her head to roll with the kneading of Tourmaline's fingers. "Are you afraid of dying?"

Tourmaline's voice was surprised. "Not any more."

"Not your body," *said Francie.* "I mean you."

"My mind?" *Francie didn't answer. Tourmaline continued,* "I'll think about it eventually."

"I've thought," *said Francie,* "and I'm afraid."

"Then for now, forget it."

"My father, did you know him?"

"No."

"He was too old for the treatments," *said Francie,* "but he lived well into his second century. As he grew older, something happened with his mind."

"Senility."

"That's it. He stayed with us and I watched him every day. I had to be extraordinarily quiet, or he would become upset. At times he didn't know me."

Tourmaline stroked Francie's hair soothingly. "Wasn't it a peaceful and gentle decline?"

"It was decay," *said Francie, beginning to weep and muffling her voice in the plush towel.* "He was buried when he was a hundred and thirty. My father died long before that."

Tourmaline kissed Francie gently. "Don't think about it," *she said again.* "Don't think."

Jack Burton intimidates. More than two meters tall, the Network star is proportionately muscled, and that muscle tissue is in exquisite tone. He does all his

own stunt work. Only his flame-red hair is fake. Burton
has backed Francie and Kandelman into a corner.
Drunkenly, gait unsteady, he perorates:

"So I told them at the Network, 'Goddammit, guys,
this is the best script we've picked up in the century.
It's got drama, it's got meaning, it's got—goddammit
—true seriousness.' You know what those bastards
said?"

"No," Francie says, bored.

"Mannie!" Kandelman yells. "Get over here."

"They said," Burton continues. "They said . . .
you won't believe what they said. The bastards."

Kandelman peeks past Burton's shoulder. "Goddammit, Mannie!"

"The bastards said it'd hurt my image."

Francie giggles. "We love your image, Jack."

"After all the shit melodrama. This was going to
be *something*. A complete turning point for me—I
mean, for the character. But the Network—"

Mannie arrives, agent, manager, keeper, lover.
He puts his manicured hand on Burton's arm. "Party's over, Jack. Time to go home."

Burton's eyes widen maniacally, staring at the
pair in the corner. He ignores Mannie. "The realiza-
tion, you know? All cells in the body can regenerate.
Anything can be renewed. Anything but brain cells."

Mannie's grip tightens. "Come on, Jack."

"An epiphany: when they die, they die. Forever,
goddammit."

"Forget it," says Mannie. "Now come on."

"Forever." Burton's chin drops, the animation
leaves his face. He begins to weep softly. Mannie, short
and burly, leads Jack Burton away like a draft animal.
They disappear in the crowd.

"Cortex," says Francie. "Gray matter." She
dredges the shibboleths from some vagrant memory,
then looks brightly up at Kandelman for approval.

"Cerebrum," says Kandelman sourly.

Francie doesn't really understand the game.
"What?"

"Forget it." He stares speculatively at her breasts.
"Come on. Let's go for a drive."

The party pavilion smolders with the muted colors of a thousand simulated tropical birds. Over the crowd-mutter sounds the whir of wings. Francie and Kandelman exit between twin columns of whirling doves. Feather-light touches brush against clothing.

Sternig watches. His jealousy is deeply embedded. The pair disappears beyond the pavilion and Sternig turns back to Tourmaline and his ever-present drink. Aware of her eyes, he frowns self-consciously. Her face betrays no judgment.

Yes, there was a time. . . . When was it, he wonders, or when will it be. A time, together . . .

> They hired a room, not on the water this time, but at an inn near the desert. They spent an hour wandering among the dunes. Francie wore her sunsuit, narrow yellow bands across the mahogany of her flesh, dark woodstain skin that took on an added sheen of sweat.
>
> She laughed and rolled down a slope, coming up at the dune's base with her skin lightly dusted with sand. She brushed the grit away from her eyes. "Let's go back to the room," she said. "I want a shower."
>
> Out of the languorous heat, bodies clean oiled, they made love. Francie shrieked and thrashed and bit and moaned and sucked and scratched. Eventually, during a quietus, he asked her if it had been good, and she, hesitating a long minute, finally answered, no, not exactly. He asked why not and she replied that she was never quite satisfied. He prodded for details. She attempted to explain.
>
> "Sisyphic orgasm," he mused aloud.
>
> She wanted to know what that meant so he began to explain the legend. She grew bored and touched his body, again hungry. He stopped talking and tried to kiss each millimeter of her skin.
>
> Finally—again—she drew back shuddering from the brink.

*As he was about to drift into sleep,
Francie asked him to tell her something beautiful.*

*"There is no greater sorrow than to recall, in misery, the time when we were
happy."*

"That's pretty."

"It's Dante," he said.

"Poor Sternig," says Tourmaline."

"Don't pity me."

"I don't. I hate pity. I'm only concerned."

Sternig scowls and says, "Don't be concerned
about me."

She ruffles his hair slightly, as though he were a
child, then runs an index finger along the underline
of his jaw. "I like you, Sternig. You remind me of an
ancient friend. I hate to see you hurting yourself, replaying old mistakes again and again."

"What happened to your friend?"

"Metaphorically dead," says Tourmaline flatly. "I
think. Maybe he's mad and locked away somewhere.
Or mad and running loose."

Sternig says, "I know what I'm doing."

"No," she says, "you don't. You may think you do."

"You think I should forget about Francie."

"Yes," she says patiently. "Yes. That's it."

"And if I don't?"

"You'll lose your mind, your soul; whatever,
you'll lose it."

Sternig says thoughtfully, "I don't know."

Her brow creases with exasperation and anger.
"Sternig, get off the carousel!"

Back-seat sex, adolescence recollected in senility.
Kandelman wheels Francie's car onto an eroded bluff
overlooking the sea. Tonight the water is glassy. For a
brief time they stare at the reflected stars extending
out to the horizon.

Francie's gambit: "It's awfully beautiful."

Kandelman inwardly winces. "No more so than
you."

"No talking," says Francie. "Please love me." She lies across the seat so her head settles in Kandelman's lap. She wonders when she last used the spray and how she smells.

Kandelman touches her hair, lifts her face toward him, kisses her tenderly at first, then harder. She lies back and he begins to massage her body, starting with her thighs. Tiny ainimal cries come from Francie's throat; she shivers as though with a chill. Kandelman's fingers stroke and stroke. He will save those wondrous breasts for the last, a gourmet dessert.

But when he does touch those breasts, naked to his eyes for the first time, his hands freeze in mid-motion. He again tentatively touches the breasts. And again stops.

Eyes closed, Francie says, "What's wrong?"

"They don't feel right," says Kandelman.

Francie opens her eyes. "Don't you like them?"

"They look great. But there's something—"

"I had them fixed just for you," cries Francie.

"Such a strange feel." Kandelman gingerly touches her with a finger.

Francie says angrily. "They're fine. They're nonallergenic. They're the best alloplastics I could—"

Kandelman interrupts. "They're not right. Something unnatural—"

"The niples are electrostimulating. They're wired to—"

"I want a woman," says Kandelman.

Francie resorts to tears and Kandelman strokes her hair. She stops crying abruptly, raises her head, and extends an investigatory hand. "No," she says. "Don't go soft on me."

He tries to pass it off wittily, but fumbles. While the silence lengthens, he stares out at the ocean. After a minute or two, he says, "How about a little game of sniff 'n' whiff?"

"Fuck you," she says.

Silence resumes until Kandelman, uncomfortable, shifts his position. Francie sighs, sits erect, and gazes out the window.

"Let's go back to the party."

The dance floor seems suspended in night. Tourmaline and Sternig sit at a table on the periphery. Cou-
ples drift past; groups, an occasional single.

"Sponge and renewal," says Tourmaline. They've
been talking of the past again. "But time wears deeply.
We tend to keep our lives in endless repetitions. The
grooves are too deeply etched. It takes a supreme act
of will to break free."

"I don't have that will," Sternig says. "I know that
now."

"You knew that before. I can remember. Can't
you?"

He looks at her mutely.

"How can you know," she asks, "but still not act
on it?"

Sternig sees Francie waiting on the opposite side
of the dance floor. She waves to him. He stands and
looks bleakly down at Tourmaline. "Next time around,
help me? Please?" He stammers slightly.

"Next time around," she says. "We can try."

Sternig leaves her. Halfway across the floor, he
stops among the whirling dancers and smiles briefly and
sadly back at Tourmaline.

She watches Francie and Sternig disappear in the
dark. What she says is, "People receive the kind of
lovers they deserve," but she knows she doesn't feel
that. Tourmaline sighs; then scans the party crowd,
seeking out the clean beauty of Marlene's bright hair.

4

The
Legend
of
Cougar
Lou
Landis

The gardener Yakov lay dying in the desert gravel. He sprawled on his left side, eyes to the east, where he watched the stars blur above Cinnabar. Oh, for warmth. Was this how it was to die of cold? Yakov had always believed freezing to be a slow decline into gentle sleep. There was first the sharp bite of frost, yes. But then came the sleepy arrival of death. Not for Yakov; he had lain alert for hours. The gravel chafed his skin unbearably. The beating administered him by his master had broken bones. Yakov moaned softly and prayed the cold to kill.

There was an answer on the wind. Yakov listened intently. Was it his master, returning to inflict more pain? Yakov tried to pull gravel over himself, to darken the shadows in which he hid. The wind brought the voice again, closer this time. "Is someone there? Who is it?"

Yakov pulled at the small rocks with his one good hand. He whimpered in spite of himself.

"I hear you. You're at the foot of the dune. What's the matter?"

A figure rose up in the night and bent over him. Frightened, Yakov flinched and closed his eyes. Hair softly tickled across his face.

"You're hurt, aren't you?" Fingers gently touched the gardener's shattered limbs.

Yakov opened his eyes and blinked, trying to focus. "Who are you?"

"I'm a friend." The voice was low and sympathetic. The woman's fingers continued to probe carefully. "Lie perfectly still."

"It hurts very much," said Yakov.

"*. . . hurts very much.*"

"*Is it worth the pain?*" *said her mother.*

She stared at her hands, flexing the fingers repeatedly; then made a fist. She extended the index finger and brought it slowly toward her nose. The finger touched her upper lip and she recoiled. "It's worth the pain," she affirmed. "The strangeness is something else again."

"I think you're dying."

"I know. I've wanted to die for hours."

"You're cold," said the woman. She pulled a piece of clothing, soft and warm, over Yakov. She flicked a lighter. "I'm afraid there's no kindling for a fire out here."

Yakov stared at her face. "I know you. I've heard of you. You're Cougar Lou." With a tired wonder he looked at her long, tawny hair and wide, violet eyes. Then the flame went out. "Will you help me?"

"You know that you're dying."

"I want vengeance."

"Who did this?"

"Josephus the Administrator. I worked in his greenhouse. His favorite orchids were the flaming moths. Somehow they died of rust. Josephus was furious."

"The son of a bitch," said Cougar Lou.

"I think it's getting colder."

"I wish I had more than my cape. I'm sorry."

"I'm glad I met you." Yakov choked on the blood and twisted his head aside to spit.

"Would you like that bastard to die?"

The operating theater glittered like sunlight on snow. She felt like dying; then remembered how soon, how grandly she would live.

Yakov made a twisted smile in the darkness.

"Now lie back," said Cougar Lou. "I can make it easier for you."

Yakov coughed rackingly. He brought his knees up in the foetal position. "Too late . . ."

"No," she said. "Here." Cougar Lou pressed a metal cube tightly against the gardener's temple. His body spasmed.

```
Yakov the gardener:
   akov the gardener: B
    kov the gardener: Br
     ov the gardener: Bro
      v the gardener: Bros
        the gardener: Brosk
        the gardener: Broskl
       he gardener: Broskla
        e gardener: Brosklaw
          gardener: Brosklaw
         ardener: Brosklaw t
          rdener: Brosklaw th
           dener: Brosklaw the
            ener: Brosklaw the
             ner: Brosklaw the c
              er: Brosklaw the ch
               r: Brosklaw the chi
                : Brosklaw the chie
                  Brosklaw the chief
```

It broke open, pushed free, gulped alien air, and wished somatically for the soothing liquid to return. Wailing, the baby was slapped, bathed, wrapped, and rocked. Later, it fed.

"Do!" he said, pointing. A proud voice: "He said it; his first word."

Another time, the second word: "Get!"

The pride of parents: so precious, so bright. "We love you." And they rocked him every time he cried.

"Brosie, Brosie," said playmate Kenneth. "Little baby Brosie." Kenneth was twice Brosklaw's size; Brosklaw hit him with a rock.

"Brosklaw, you will go far," said his mother.

"Listen to your mother," said his father.

They pushed him, stimulated him with books and tapes and holos. Not too much music, though. Very little art. He became extremely capable and knowledgeable, and even suspected how good he really was.

"Brosklaw, you will go far," said his tutor. "Just continue to apply yourself."

By adolescence, he retained a long string of lovers.

"Sometimes I wonder what I'm doing here with you," mused Tourmaline Hayes, the sex star. "Morbid curiosity?"

He laughed and made love to her again.

"Only the best education," said his father. "Selden University."

"The police?" said his mother.

"Real power is the control of human behavior," quoted her son.

"You've got everything you want," said each of his wives at one time or another. "What more?"

"I have everything I wanted," he corrected them. "As I grow older I discover new things to desire."

"Chief of Police of Craterside Park," his mother said, during a visit. "That's impressive for one so young."

Brosklaw smiled.

His mother said, "When will you move up to city administration?"

"That's coming."

Brosklaw walked down one of the clean, well-lighted streets of Craterside Park. A woman stepped from between two spiral towers and confronted him. He stared at the lithe body. "Don't I know you?" he said. "You're—"

Yakov the gardener shook convulsively a final time and died. Cougar Lou took the cold piece of metal away from his head. She retrieved her cape and watched him for a while. In the starlight, Yakov was barely visible against the gravel.

". . . *rather be anybody than who I am.*" She looked defiantly at her mother.

"*Your adolescence has been prolonged,*" said Anita.

She picked up a film-viewer and hurled it at the wall. The viewer exploded in a thousand shining pieces.

"*Don't do that,*" said Anita mildly. *She put her hand to the cut on her forehead and one finger came away red.*

Cougar Lou shivered and rubbed her hands together. They were sticky with Yakov's blood. It was real, and the smell of it made her sick.

The quiet of a Craterside Park night was shattered by the sound of a man attacking a sculpture in one of the district's many scenic parks. The statue was the heroic stylization of a mastodon. Its massive feet were anchored solidly in a base. It could not move, other than to wind its trunk back and squirt water at its attacker. The man leaned against the statue's haunch, repeatedly driving a fist into its ribs. The sound boomed hollowly. The sculpture honked in distress and discharged another ineffective stream.

Eventually, Craterside Park residents anonymously contacted the police. A patrol car whispered up to the square and set down. The two cops approached the mastodon's assailant warily.

"Hey!" said the short cop. "Stop that. Turn around and keep your hands in plain sight."

The second patrolman hefted his stunner, just in case.

The man slowly turned at the cop's voice. He stared at the patrolmen vaguely. Hulking, he was at least a head taller than either cop.

"Easy," warned the first cop. "Take it slow."

They shined their lights in the man's face.

The first cop gasped. "Chief Brosklaw? Is that you?"

"Chief?" said the second cop. He took a step closer.

"Chief?" echoed the man. "Chief?" His jaw hung slack. He turned back to the stylized mastodon and again began to pound its flank, the boom resounding far across Craterside Park.

Mary Elouise Olvera-Landis returned home quite early in the morning. She let herself into the huge old house on Feldspar Drive quietly. Only one of her contract husbands greeted her. "Are Nels and Richard asleep?" she asked.

Macy got up from the couch in front of the fireplace and stretched. "They didn't last past midnight."

Lou kissed him. She tried to play no favorites, but Macy held an edge in her affections. He was the practical one of her husbands, thinking rather than feeling. She often sensed he was troubled, as though trying to find his way out of imaginary labyrinths. Richard, her first husband, was undisciplined and lustful. She found him exciting. The second, Nels, was ethereally worshipful, but usually preoccupied with his researches at the Tancarae Institute.

"Where have you been?"

"Out," she said.

"Cards at your family's?"

She put her hands to her throat and unbuckled the cape. "I took the windhover out to the greenbelt. I wanted to walk alone in the desert."

Smiling, he said, "Did you find a burning bush?" Macy was a librarian and knew all the old stories.

She shook her head. "I found a dying man."

"Anyone we know?"

"Don't joke," she snapped. "He was a stranger."

"I thought it might be your flair for drama."

She nodded. "You're right; it was a fiction. Forget it."

"Do you want a drink?"

"Something hot. No stimulants."

They sat by the fireplace and drank mint tea. "How long until morning?" Lou asked.

"Three hours, maybe four."

"I want to sleep here by the fireplace."

"Carpet's filthy. Nels didn't clean yesterday."

"He forgot," Lou said.

"Well, it's still dirty."

"I'll put my cape down," she mocked. "Do you mind?"

"I'm not finicky." He reached for her. She allowed him to draw her down. After they had made love, the artificial logs still burned brightly. "Turn down the fire." said Macy sleepily.

Lou twisted the valve. "Are you tired?"

"Yes." He nuzzled against her like a child, left leg thrown over her waist.

"I'm not sleepy."

He opened one eye. "What do you want?"

She smiled ingenuously. "A story."

Macy groaned and sat up. "Once upon a time, there was a brave woman named Robin Hood . . ."

In the dim light of the fireplace, Macy looked exasperated. "Aren't you tired yet?"

She shook her head.

"You're worse than any child. All right, what do you want to talk about?"

"Anything."

He considered. "Since I'm the newest of your husbands, let's talk about you."

"All right."

"There's a hologram in your room. Is that your sister?"

She was quiet for a few moments. "I didn't expect that."

"You don't have to answer."

"The hologram is not my sister. It's me."

His voice was surprised. "She looks nothing like you."

"For convenience," the surgeon said, *"we have standard patterns."*

She shook her head. *"I brought my own specifications."*

"The family's prosperous," said Lou. "We can purchase wonders. Have you any idea what I was like as a child?"

"You were extroverted, bright, and athletic. I imagine you were the center of all interest here in Craterside Park."

"Wrong. I was bright, but I was also clumsy and fat. I was introverted to the point of catatonia. Months and months I wouldn't go out of the house. I spent my time reading and viewing heroic fantasies—Joan of Arc, Robin Hood, Gerry Cornelius, all of them. I imagined I was all sorts of other people living in different times."

"Escapist."

"Didn't you ever dream?"

"Of course."

"Of what?"

He considered the question. "I don't remember."

"I dreamed I was a hero. I saw myself as strong and lithe as a cougar. One birthday, my parents gave me all that. It took months for the restructuring. Months more for physical training."

Macy looked intrigued. "That holo—the difference is incredible."

"Sometimes I wish I were her again."

"That's stupid." He gently kissed a line along her jaw. "You're beautiful now."

"Would you feel that if I were still her?"

He hesitated. "I think so."

"You only approach honesty." She laughed. "You're so damned political."

"Beautiful Cougar Lou."

"What?" Startled.

"You dreamed of being a cougar. Cougar Lou. It fits."

"It does," Lou murmured, almost as a question. "It's almost morning. Let's make love again."

Before sunrise, they moved to the tall windows facing east.

Better than lying with a book in an invented world?

He raised his head. "Did you say something?"

She shook her head slowly. "Do you know," said Macy, "that you talk in your sleep?"

The elder matriarch of the Olvera-Landis family arrived shortly after noon. Lou greeted her mother at the door.

"Good afternoon, Mary Elouise," said Anita. "Are your husbands about?"

"Macy is out," Lou said. "Nels is at the Institute and Richard is with a party hunting for sea snark."

"Fine. I wish to talk with you alone." She led Lou to the parlor. "This is nothing you haven't heard before."

"I expected that."

"The family has been talking," said Anita. "We are worried about you. Don't you think that perhaps this house is a little large for you to manage?"

"I have three husbands."

"And aren't they also perhaps a bit too much?"

"I can manage."

"Can you really, dear?" She placed a plump hand on her daughter's wrist. "You are young and wilful, Mary Elouise, but that will carry you only so far. What are you going to *do*?"

"I'll live here." Lou stared at the carpet, following patterns. "I intend to help people."

"Heroes?" Macy once laughed. "Heroines? Killers and thieves—outlaws."

In a rage, she ordered him from her bed.

Anita laughed. "My dear, machines are for helping people. People have better things to do."

Lou kept a stubborn silence.

"The family is reluctant to continue supporting you in this fashion. You've had a nice fling. Now come home."

"Into the family business?"

"If you'd like. We won't force you."

"And my husbands?"

"Three seem a bit extravagant. Can't you keep—" She rolled her shoulders. "Oh, just one?"

"*So will you marry me?*"

"*The terms are good,*" said Macy. "*Why not?*"

"*Is that all?*"

"*This isn't* Le Morte d'Arthur, *love.*"

"Mother, may I think about it?"

"Again? I suppose so. But you'll have to return soon. The expense, you know. Supporting a separate house in Craterside Park is so ridiculous. You can't expect these birthday extravagances to last forever."

"I realize that."

"Then I'll talk to you again soon." Anita rose to leave. "Oh, did you hear about our fine police chief?"

"What about him?"

"I saw it on Network this morning. He was picked up by his own men last night. He attempted to damage a nocturnal sculpture in one of the squares."

"How odd," said Lou.

"Indeed. Even stranger, it seems his entire memory is gone. The police suspect foul play."

"Craterside Park used to be so peaceful."

Her mother agreed. "These days, I don't know what we're coming to."

After Anita left, Lou went to her special room. No one slept with her there. It was a retreat. The floor undulated over circulating liquid. The walls opened into infinitely expanded holovistas. Today, Lou chose trees. She was surrounded by brooding, illusory forests. She lay down on the forest floor.

How blessed to rest. She still dreamed as Cougar Lou, but when she woke, could not remember those dreams.

She dozed, but did not sleep; and came awake disoriented and confused. She stared at the underbrush, wishing that once, just once, an unprogramed animal would come slinking out to greet her. Lou turned over and watched clouds traverse the high-resolution blue sky.

Steal from the rich, give to the poor. . . . That had come from Macy and the dusty, tattered pages of an ancient book.

What am I doing, she thought. How can I re-create a past that probably never existed? Whom am I helping helping helping helping . . .

Wake up, wake up, whispered the night wind. Lou jerked upright. "All right," she said. "I'm awake." The forests blinked out and Lou was alone in the small gray room.

Outside, Nels waited for her. He was clearly agitated. "I'm sorry," he said. "I thought you ought to know. Macy and Richard are fighting."

She rubbed her eyes. "What about?"

"You."

"I'm still asleep," Lou said. "Why should they fight over me?"

"Come on," said Nels. He tugged her toward the hallway.

"Why me?"

Nels stumbled over the words. "It's your family. We heard you're going back. You'll keep only one husband—"

"Let's go." They hurried along the corridor, Nels' bony legs pacing her. "Who told you?"

Nels looked at her uncomfortably. "It was my cousin Ingrid. Her maid's aunt is second housekeeper to the Olvera-Landis household. The aunt heard a discussion about you at dinner and couldn't keep it to herself." He ducked his head. "I'm sorry. I told Richard; then he and Macy got into it."

"They're idiots," Lou said.

They clattered down the main stairs. Richard and Macy were in the dining hall. The table had been shoved to one side and the two men stood in the cleared space. Each was clad only in a pair of baggy white pantaloons, tied securely at waist and ankles. The two men jumped up and down, screaming epithets.

Lou stopped at the bottom of the flight. She wondered whether to laugh. "What are they doing?"

"Their pantaloons," Nels said, pointing. "Each of them dropped a resurrectronic ferret in there. The first one whose ferret gnaws its way free through the cloth wins."

"That's stupid!" Lou cried. She ran into the dining hall and grabbed Macy's shoulder. Without taking his eyes from Richard's face, he shoved her aside.

"Leave us be," said Richard. He was stocky, with long arms and head as smooth as a desert stone.

High-pitched squeaks came from the men's trousers.

"Idiots!" Lou screamed. "When the ferrets are through, neither of you'll be fit to be a husband!"

"Get away," said Macy. "We have to settle it. First us; then Nels."

"Nels, help me stop them." Lou grabbed one of the spindly dining room chairs and smashed it at a suspicious bulge on Macy's calf. Her husband yelled and fell sidewise. Something jerked and twitched under the fabric of his pantaloons. Lou swung again with the broken chair leg and heard sophisticated circuitry break.

"Damn you," said Macy. He reached to stop her hand. She kicked him in the face.

Lou turned and found Nels and Richard rolling on the floor. Nels' legs were locked around Richard's waist. Jack-knifed forward, he pummeled a lump on Richard's ankle.

"Richard! It's over." Her first husband glared up at her; then took his hands away from Nels' throat.

The four people surveyed each other. Macy wiped his bloody nose with his hand Lou gave him a napkin from the sideboard. Nels massaged his own throat gingerly. Richard sat up, looking sullen.

"You stupid pricks," said Lou. "Is Nels the only one with any sense?"

"It's true, then? You're going back to your faily?" Richard demanded.

"Who gets discarded?" said Macy.

"Anita came to see me today. That's what she wanted."

"So what are you going to do?"

"I haven't decided. But I do know I don't want you fighting over me like stud bulls."

"Aren't you the great romantic?" Macy said spitefully.

Lou turned on him. "No, not this way. Now all of you, get out. Just leave me alone."

The three men stared at her. "Do you want to see any of us later on tonight?" Richard asked.

She shook her head. "I'm sore and I want to be alone." Lou turned back toward the stairs. They watched until she disappeared past the upper landing.

She sat on the topmost parapet of the highest turret of the old house and dangled her feet into space. She drew the cloak about herself. The simulated cougar fur was proof against the night wind off the ocean.

Who am I, she thought. I'm Cougar Lou Landis.

No, replied Mary Elouise Olvera-Landis. I'm an ugly, awkward girl who finds only vicarious marvels. My heroes are in books and tapes and story computers. I am locked inside a walking fantasy. But that doesn't change me. I'm still Mary Elouise.

I'm the new reality, thought Cougar Lou. I exist in my strength and grace.

You will always be Mary Elouise, answered Mary Elouise.

No. No?

Cougar Lou stared out toward City Center where the stars twinkled faster and became a blur. Tomorrow, she thought, Anita will return for me. I'm such a child; I'll do as she asks.

I wish I were the hero I've pretended.

The scattered lights of Craterside Park spread below her. One of the tiny stars marked the home of Josephus the Administrator. "Yakov," she whispered. "Little gardener, you're my last chance for self-respect."

Cougar Lou stood and balanced easily on the stone parapet. . . . *steps. Stairs were the hardest. At first, the new perspectives came slowly. She stepped or reached, and often missed. The fine, lithe body throbbed with new bruises.* She looped one end of a line around a crenelation and knotted it. Then she tossed the coil into the darkness. She clipped the rope around the break-bar secured to her belt, then looped the rope around her hips and began to rappel silently down from the tower.

As a young girl, she had attended garden parties at Josephus' estate. Cougar Lou knew the route. She took alleyways and climbed over rooftops, avoiding Craterside Park's safe streets.

Two patrolmen sat telling each other ghost stories beside the gateway to Josephus' estate. ". . . out of the closet, jaws gaping . . ." The words floated across as she crawled through the shrubbery.

Cougar Lou anticipated little difficulty in getting to Josephus. There would be few safeguards. Craterside Park was relatively free of wrongdoing. The patrolmen patrolled because Chief Brosklaw had liked good appearances.

Once past the gateway, she ran across the checkerboard lawns. She reached the back of the house. A window turned silently inward and Cougar Lou let herself into Josephus' kitchen. Pausing to orient herself to the new darkness, she searched back through her adolescence and remembered the master bedroom was on the second floor, south wing. Negotiating the stairs and hallways took a few minutes. Soon she was in front of the correct door. She slid it aside and took a cold metal cube from her belt-pouch.

". . . brought us memories of a better life. Why?"

She looked away from twisted limbs and shriveled souls. "You've never had riches."

They stared at her.

Lights glared on. Across the room, Josephus sat up in bed and smiled at her. "Mary Elouise, how nice to see you. You were expected."

Cougar Lou whirled, but the hallways were filled with black-uniformed patrolmen, stunners in hand. She turned back to the bedroom, ready to break past Josephus and dive through a window.

The Administrator raised his hand and she saw the wand of a stunner. "You must be tired. Sleep now, and we'll talk in the morning." She felt a momentary sting, then nothing else.

Mary Elouise awoke slowly. She stared at the dark, slender man and wondered who he was. The woman beside him also looked familiar. She blinked and realized the woman was her mother. The man was Josephus. She whimpered and tried to roll over, to go back to sleep. Josephus grasped her shoulders and shook her.

"Have some tea, dear," said her mother. They waited while she sat up and drank. After several minutes, her eyes focused and she put down the cup.

"Anita?"

"You're home, dear. Josephus brought you in quite early. It appears you've been bad."

Josephus chuckled. He upended his palm and three metal cubes rolled onto the table. "Memory cubes. You planned to use one on me?"

"It was for Yakov," Mary Elouise said. "I promised."

"For whom?" said Anita.

"My former gardener, an incompetent. I was rather harsh on him." He fingered the cubes. "Stolen memories. . . . There was Brosklaw, of course. Who else? We've had several reports."

"There were three more; a woman, two men. They were lucky people with power and accomplishments. They were gifts of birth. I gave their memories to cripples I found wandering out beyond the greenbelt."

Anita pursed her lips. "You've been a very bad girl."

"Me?" Cougar Lou glared. "Don't condescend like that. I'm not a girl anymore."

Josephus slapped his palm down hard on the table and laughed. "Who is condescending? Do you think that murder by memory-theft and the gift of those memories to persons you deem less fortunate isn't condescending?"

"No."

"Child, you've got a lot to learn."

"What are you going to do?"

Anita said, "You must be disciplined."

"Punished," said Josephus. "It's an ugly word, but it's more what I had in mind."

"The steel rod?"

"Nothing so brutal. You must realize that memory retrieval holds a good deal more than the historical romances you absorbed for so long. You'll experience some of the less pleasant memories. My special selection."

"You disgust me," said Cougar Lou.

Josephus grinned again. "I think about a thousand subjective years will be appropriate. Then you'll get your old body back."

"I'd already decided that."

"What do you mean?"

Cougar Lou smiled; then the smile slowly diminished. "You were waiting. How did you know?"

"How do you think?"

They took her out then, and in the hall her three husbands were waiting.

"Which one of you sons of bitches was it?" Cougar Lou demanded. "Who betrayed me?" She glared at Nels. "You? You got me the cubes from the Institute."

"It could be any one of us," said Macy. "Or all. You talk in your sleep."

"Was it you?"

"Who's to know which you would have rejected?" Macy spread his hands noncommittally. "It doesn't matter. Who loved you more? To whom would betrayal matter the most?"

"It matters the most to me."

"From what book did you steal that?" said Macy.

She stared at him until he looked away. "No book," said Cougar Lou. "My life." Josephus reached for her elbow, to lead her out; she jerked free.

5

Hayes
and
the
Heterogyne

On November 22, 1963, a sixteen-year-old University of Denver student was run down and metaphorically killed by a speeding time machine. By "killed," it is not meant he suffered a condition either literal or permanent. The student, whose name was Harry Vincent Blake, was effectively severed from his own here-and-now and transferred somewhere else. Some*when* else. That's death.

The odor of insulation burning.

A metallic, acid taste in the back of his throat.

The sound of a ripsaw biting and binding in wet lumber.

He hadn't really been aware of the library's hushed ambiance. The musty scent of the stacks was too familiar to consciously note. Vince Blake had been preoccupied, mentally reviewing again his notes in preparation for a quiz in his zoology lab. He stepped into the revolving door and put out his hands. His fingers touched nothing; he fell forward ... and forward ...

More like rubber tires aflame, the smell.

The taste in his throat was vomit.

The ripsaw whine found a companion set of harmonics.

Back in the Mary Reed Library, no one had

looked at the revolving door; no one had marked the entrance, or the lack of an exit. The girl at the check-out desk thumbed up the volume on the radio and startled faces turned toward her. "Oh my God!" some-one said.

Tourmaline Hayes and Timnath Obregon had re-cently finished making love in the latter's laboratory. They lay loosely entwined on one of the broad tables in the experimental section, with the gear scooted down to one end to make a comfortable space. Obregon and Hayes were old friends who valued their intermittent, if often stormy, periods of companionship.

"Tired?"

"Sex with you is always such a celebration," said Obregon.

"That's what makes me a star," Tourmaline said. "Is it a criticism?"

"No, just a comment. Maybe a codification and reaffirmation."

"All that?" Her laugh was low and musical. She lightly ran her fingernails down the taut skin of his rib cage.

"Don't do that. I still have work to do."

"What's the project?"

"This week I'm inventing time travel."

She trailed her nails lower, along his belly. "Some-times you're one of the most grandiose people with whom I've ever made love. You like to astonish me with revelations. Time travel, really?"

Obregon moaned something that could either have been assent or pleasure. He carefully detached her hand. "Really."

She replaced her fingers and exerted small pres-sures. "Once, in one of my bored periods, I took an early-morning Network course in temporal physics. The professor pretty much destroyed the case for practical time travel."

Obregon said distractedly, "That's the problem with popular science. No imagination." Again he brushed away her hand.

And again she replaced it. "I know. That's why

my curiosity occasionally brings me here to the Institute. Did you think I come merely for the benefit of your flaccid attentions?"

They both laughed. Obregon said, "Time travel exists. You see evidence of it all around you in Cinnabar."

"*I* do?"

He suddenly sat up, levering himself on bony elbows. "Look at the very nature of the vortical time streams that converge on the city. In City Center the times belts move appreciably faster than the belts further out toward the suburbs. The city is so huge, one doesn't always notice. But the difference becomes apparent when one moves from one belt to another."

"Don't lecture me," Tourmaline said, giving him a cautionary squeeze. "That I can get from the Network."

Obregon winced. "Sorry. Sometimes I forget I'm not a pedant anymore."

"Not officially. I suspect you amuse yourself in private by devising declamations."

"Listen, do you want to know about time travel or not?"

Mock-chastened, "Yes, I want to know about time travel."

"Then consider this. A person moving toward City Center on a straight line would effectively be approaching the future. Each concentric time belt toward the center would accelerate him forward."

"Toward what?"

"That's theoretical. At the precise center, presumably the final collapse and regeneration of the universe."

"All right, but that's not *time travel*. I'm talking about someone actually traveling into her own past or future."

"What I'm talking about is a matter of perspective," said Obregon. "I'm merely pointing out that time distortions exist right here at home where we can observe them."

"Don't be sulky," Tourmaline said. She bent forward and let her blue hair sweep slowly across his upper thighs.

Obregon mumbled something.

"What?"

"I suspect you're not really interested in time travel."

"But I am, Timnath." She put her hands on his shoulders and drew him inexorably down beside her. "I would enjoy traveling through time. How long before your vehicle is perfected?"

"I have no vehicle."

"Then—?" She straddled him carefully.

With resignation he said, "I'm running a time-trawling experiment. This is the initial phase; actual time-traversing gadgets will come later. It takes time to erect a program."

"Doesn't it, though," said Tourmaline, situating herself. Obregon put his hands on her waist. "I'm disappointed. Then there's no beautiful gingerbread machine like the one about which I read in that marvelous Mr. Wells?"

"No." He let his fingers stroke along her flanks. "It's as though I've encountered a wide river but haven't invented the boat. I'm standing on the bank with ropes and grappling hooks. I can see debris washing by, and some of it I can retrieve from the shore. But I still can't venture out in my own craft."

Tourmaline contracted her muscles and felt his back arch in response. "That's an awful metaphor. The professor on the Network program said that comparing time to a river was the oldest cliché in temporal mechanics."

Obregon made gasping, pleasured noises.

"Articulate, Timnath."

"I said use any simile you like. Time fits almost any image you can think of. Oh. *Ohhh.*"

"Time is like . . . the water vanishing down a sink drain."

"Banal." He lifted his hands to cup her breasts. "Basically correct, but too ordinary."

"Time is like . . . a ripe, spotted banana."

"Don't be silly."

She began to laugh. "Time is like . . . a frog's tongue."

Obregon's distracted features composed for a moment. "That's right. That's truly accurate. How did you know?"

"Know—what?" said Tourmaline. Her eyes looked at him but they were not focused.

Obregon rocked beneath her. "You know," laughing, breath hissing between clenched teeth, "you know you know."

Beyond them, a bell chimed softly.

"It worked!" Obregon tried to sit up, bumping his forehead against Tourmaline's chin. His expression was suddenly intent.

"What are you doing?"

The bell chimed again, three times. "It *worked.*" Obregon disengaged himself, swinging one leg down off the table.

"Timnath, you—" Her voice shook. "You *fool*! What—"

He grabbed her hand and nearly dragged her from the table. "Come on, it's the alarm. Something in the time stream—my devices have locked onto it."

"Timnath!" Her voice approached a wail.

They stumbled across the laboratory. "We may have captured the first time traveler," said Obregon.

"Fuck," said Tourmaline.

Vince Blake fell through the pearl-gray medium which had no other identifying sensory characteristics. It was neither warm nor cold, with no odors and no sounds. The only thing to watch was his companion, the two-by-three-foot breadboard assemblage, winking and sparkling its circuitry atop a cubical black box. Vince had no idea what the machine was, though he'd spent considerable time speculating. The machine orbited him slowly; but its perigee was about a yard, and that was not close enough for Vince to reach across the intervening space.

Subjective time dilated.

**27. (Q) The process of sexual reproduction
in the genus Paramecium is called
_____.**

(A) Conjugation.

His spatial orientation was minimal; confusion
stymied attempts to assign labels to up or down or sidewise. Yet Vince knew he fell. He had tried sky-diving
the previous summer and this was how it felt, though
without the rush of wind tearing at his clothing. *Free
fall,* he thought. *Is this how it was for Colonel Glenn?*
But free fall in—what? English 412, last quarter. He
recalled Alice's interminable tumble down the rabbit
hole.

**79. (Q) Why does the male opossum have a
forked penis?**
(A) Because the female has two vaginas.

Vince's sense of time was stalled. Occasionally he
checked his watch, but the hands remained poised invariably at 1:28. He couldn't remember whether it had
been morning or evening.

**192. (Q) The primary male hormones are
called _____.**
(A) Androgens.

Something important remained with him—the
constant, nagging knowledge of the importance of this
afternoon's zoology test. He had slacked off the past
few weeks . . . Karen . . . his grade hung in precarious
balance. In his mind he created questions and answered
them. Endlessly.

**460. (Q) What characteristic do female cats
and female rabbits have in com-
mon when they are in heat?**
**(A) They are both spontaneous ovula-
tors.**

And all the while, further back toward the rear
of his skull, mental Muzak endlessly replayed the Cas-

cades singing: "Listen to the rhythm of the falling rain."
He speculated whether he might have died and gone to
hell.

1,386. (Q) True or false: a male porcupine must urinate on the female to make her sexually receptive.

(A) "True," he said aloud, but heard the
sound only because the vibrations traveled from his
larynx to his ears via the intervening tissues and bones.
Sounds coming from his mouth were damped as soon
as they tried to penetrate the gray space. It gave him a
spooky feeling.

1,387. (Q) —

Piss on it, he thought—and remembered question
1,386. He grinned, and then thought of Karen, and
then dove headlong into depression. It was not a
novelty. Karen had sat beside him in the afternoon functional anatomy section for nearly a quarter now. He
had hardly dared speak to her except for the Friday
she forgot her pen and asked to borrow one of his.
Karen was beautiful, nineteen, and, for Vince, unap-
proachable. For the entire quarter she had starred in
his masturbatory fantasies. Virgin dreams.

Before Karen there had been a round-faced bru-
nette with slow, sleepy eyes named Angela. English
412. Vince had hesitantly asked her to accompany him
to the Homecoming Dance. She had turned him down
ungracefully. She had laughed. *Would I date my little
brother?* To her it was a minor matter and she never
noticed when Vince moved for the remainder of the
quarter to another row. Vince remembered and brooded
and hurt. Increasingly he regretted his being sixteen
and precocious. Pubescence was difficult.

Vince wondered what it was like to make out.

It seemed to be infinite, the number of Friday
nights he had walked through the dormitory lobby on
the way to see a movie alone. The lobby was always
crowded with guys waiting to pick up their dates. All
the swim-team jocks from New York and the baseball

jocks from Southern California. Vince watched them laugh and be cool and he wondered what it was like. This fall the big catchword in from the coasts was "bitchin'." Whenever Vince tried to use topical jargon he sounded unsure and pretentious. But since he talked to few people, perhaps it really didn't matter.

Bitchin'.

He was aware of a change in motion. He had the feeling that the alteration had been building up for some time before it was sufficiently large to notice. He still fell, but now there was a lateral force; it tugged with a steady, insistent gentleness. Physics 532, but before that, of course, Cherry Creek Junior High general science: *A body in motion tends to remain in motion unless a force is applied.* Simple. He could detect no cause for the new force. The machine with its breadboard components still circled him silently, no change in its measured orbit.

Vince felt a wave of nausea. He shut his eyes and swallowed and when he opened his eyes again, he stared. He was circling the lip of a cosmic funnel.

He felt as though he were looking miles down the inside wall of the funnel. No longer uniform, the gray lightened to a metallic sheen as it descended, then brightened to a point of painful brilliance far below in the center. Vince's eyes skipped across that point; it was like looking at the sun. His eyes watered with dazzle images.

English 412 again; Edgar Allan Poe. This was the brink of the Maelstrom. He felt himself to be an infinitesimal chip about to launch into the huge whirlpool. There were no referents; he realized he could not realistically estimate the size of the vortex below.

He saw a few dark dots on the near side of the funnel; they moved clockwise, relative to his own position. *Other flotsam?* He wondered whether they were people or machines or something else.

The lateral force pulled harder. Pain cramped his belly. He cried out and, as before, the sound died at his lips. He felt a wave of vertigo and knew he was sliding into the pit.

And it was at that point that the pain blossomed

out like a metastasis and the gray darkened to black.

When Vince awoke, two nude people were standing over him. It was the first time he'd ever seen a naked woman in the flesh.

Obregon hunkered down and touched the boy's right wrist with his fingers, seeking the pulse. "How are you—do you feel all right?"

"My stomach . . . hurts." The boy's eyes focused on Tourmaline for a moment, then looked quickly away.

"This is a time traveler?" said Tourmaline. "He's so young."

"Nausea?" said Obregon.

The boy nodded.

"With luck, that will be the worst of it." Obregon obtained a glass of effervescent liquid from the chemical console and returned to the boy's side. Tourmaline helped prop the boy's head so he could drink. Obregon took the empty glass away. "What's your name?"

"Vince. Harry Vincent Blake. Where am I?" He struggled to sit upright. "Is this a hospital?"

"This is a research laboratory at the Tancarae Institute."

"Where's that?"

"Near the suburbs of Cinnabar."

Vince said confusedly, "I was in Denver. What happened? Where's Cinnabar?"

"Timnath," said Tourmaline, "he won't look at us. What's wrong?"

Obregon said, "I think we've snagged a prude out of the time stream. Vince, does it upset you that we're naked?"

Vince's face was fiery. He mumbled something.

"How strange," said Tourmaline. "I'd better get our clothing."

Vince glanced at her and his flush improbably deepened. Tourmaline shook her blue mane in disbelief and walked away. Vince watched her swaying hips retreat. Turning back to Obregon, he repeated, "What's happened?"

"I'd hoped you'd be able to supply me with some

of those details," said Obregon. "You've been travel-ing." He pointed toward the black box crowned with the breadboard circuitry. "That brought you."

"What is it? When I started—it just seemed . . . to appear."

"It's your time machine, of course."

Vince looked bewildered. "It's not mine. I don't know what it is."

"I just told you—it's a time machine. Didn't you build it?"

"No."

"Were you merely an experimental subject for the inventor?"

"No. I told you I—"

"—am quite ignorant, I'm sure. This is indeed strange," Obregon said.

Tourmaline reentered the laboratory clad in a knee-length sapphire shift. "I hope this is modest enough." She tossed Obregon a brown, rough-woven garment.

Obregon wound the fabric around his waist and tucked in the loose end. "Do you know what a time machine is?" he said to Vince.

"I've read science fiction, but I know time ma-chines are impossible."

"I think we've been through this," said Tour-maline.

"Just accept my word that they're possible," Obre-gon said. He circled the black box, examining it. "Un-sophisticated. Apparently jury-rigged." He bent closer. "There's a metal plate screwed to the top. 'Property of Physics Department, Central Texas College of Science.'" He looked at Vince. "Is that where you came from?"

"I never heard of it. I'm a student at the Uni-versity of Denver."

"Where's that?"

"Colorado."

"Never heard of it." Obregon probed gingerly at the electronic components. "Surely this must have been a prototype."

Vince took a deep breath. "Is this the future?"

"Not for us."

"You're talking like the people in *Alice in Wonderland*." His voice and body trembling, Vince stared wildly between them. He choked on a sob.

"Baby, poor baby." Tourmaline gathered him into her arms; he pressed his face between her breasts, his back shaking as she soothed him with her fingers. "It's all right, go ahead and cry. You're all right and we're your friends." She said reproachfully to Obregon, "Give him some simple answers."

"There's no way for him to avoid cultural shock." She continued to stare at him and finally Obregon said, "I don't have any simple answers. There's too little data."

Vince blew his nose in the handkerchief Tourmaline gave him. "Have I really traveled through time?"

Obregon nodded. "It's safe to assume you're in a future relative to your embarcation point. How far a journey, I don't know. My instruments still have a limited backtrack capability. Terminex may be able to help me."

"Terminex?"

"The computer."

"I still want to know how I got here."

"As do I. My devices pulled you out of the vortical time streams."

"I remember something like a giant whirlpool." Vince's features set as though he were trying to recall the raveled threads of a nightmare. "It started to suck me down."

"The streams converge," said Obregon, "at the center of all time. And so you're here."

Abruptly, Vince said, "Can I go back?"

"I don't know."

The boy shut his eyes tightly; the muscles of his face tautened in harsh planes. His body again began to shake. Tourmaline reached toward him but Obregon restrained her wrist. After a minute, Vince took several deep, deliberate breaths and opened his eyes. He looked around the laboratory as though seeing it for the first time. "Aren't there any windows?"

"Screened," said Obregon. He clapped his hands

twice and sunlight flooded the room, gleaming and glittering on the equipment. Vince stared at the green hillside rolling down to the foot of the towers. "That's more of the Institute there, ahead of us. Off to the left you can see the first houses of Craterside Park. Look further to the side and you'll see the ocean. The desert's in back of us."

"This is the city," said Tourmaline. "Cinnabar."

Vince said, "I've been to New York and Los Angeles. I've never seen anything like this." He hesitated. "Is this the world? I mean, is this Earth?"

"We call it Earth," said Obregon. "I think home worlds are almost always called Earth."

"I wish I were home." Again, his eyes began to gleam with tears. Tourmaline touched his arm protectively.

"What's that?"

They all three looked around as the hitherto silent black box began to buzz.

"I think I'd better be alone with the time machine," said Obregon. "Will you take care of him for a while?"

Tourmaline said, "Of course."

Obregon ushered them hastily out of the laboratory. "I'll see you both later. Vince, have some food and a rest. Don't worry. Things will be fine." He smiled reassuringly.

Then the laboratory blinked out of existence and Tourmaline and Vince were alone on the hillside.

Vince extended his fingers tentatively, as though the laboratory were still there but now somehow transparent. "Where did he go?"

"Obregon? It's a little trick he uses when there's a dangerous experiment to be performed. Terminex would be extremely upset should the laboratory ever blow up and take half of Craterside Park with it."

"But how does he do it?"

"I'm not a scientist." Tourmaline shrugged. "Just a tourist."

"I don't even know your name."

"It's Tourmaline."

"That's the name of a stone. It's a pretty name."

"Thank you," said Tourmaline. "My friend's name is Timnath Obregon."

"Is he a government scientist?"

Tourmaline looked puzzled. "He's a dilettante," she said. "Just like the rest of us."

"I don't understand."

"Let's go find you a place to rest and something cold to drink." Having firmly changed the subject, Tourmaline took Vince's hand and led him down the grassy slope. Halfway to the towers, a flock of scarlet birds whirred up in their path.

"Cardinals," Vince cried. "I haven't seen any since I was in New York." His voice filled with wonder.

"How old are you?" said Tourmaline.

"Sixteen."

She looked at him sharply. *"Years?"*

"What else? How old are you?"

Tourmaline remembered Timnath's admonition about culture shock. "How old do I look?"

"Oh, maybe twenty."

"Close enough. I'm a little older."

"Twenty-five? You don't look that old."

She smiled. "Sometimes I feel it."

"You remind me of somebody I know."

"Who's that?"

"Nobody. Just a girl named Karen. You wouldn't want to hear about her."

"Of course I would, Vince."

So he told her, surprising himself by the ease with which he talked now to a stranger, especially a female stranger. He talked and she listened attentively and soon they came to a door of oiled mahogany in the base of the first tower.

"We'll go to my apartment," Tourmaline said, holding the door open for him.

Vince balked on the threshold. "It's dark in there."

She took his arm reassuringly and led him inside. "It's perfectly safe."

The disorientation was akin to his wrenching exit from the University of Denver Library. Mercifully, this

time the experience was much briefer. Vince had the
illusory feeling he was strolling down a long hallway,
but that his legs were elastic at the joints and that his
feet were preceding him by many yards. Then his feet
reached their destination and the rest of his body
caught up as though one end of a taut rubber band had
been released.

His belly twitched ominously. "My stomach
again . . ."

"It's the effect of kleining," said Tourmaline.
"Take a deep breath. You'll be fine."

There was no dark room and no dim hallway.
They stood again in sunlight, this time dappled by leaf
shadows. The tree spread its branches around and
above them. They were evidently in the middle of a
copse; Vince could see the rounded green crowns of
other trees surrounding them, but generally lower than
the platform on which they stood. The platform, sawn
from rough planks, was a disc about ten yards across.
Nested in the crotch of three limbs, each several times
as thick as Vince's body, the platform was pierced in
the center, allowing the major trunk to pass through.
Several black wrought-metal ladders and staircases evidently led to the upper reaches of the tree.

It was the most elaborate treehouse Vince had
ever seen and he said so.

"I've used it for quite a while," said Tourmaline,
"but I've never grown bored with it." She led the way
to the staircase which spiraled up around the central
trunk. "Let's go to the kitchen."

The kitchen was an oval platform projecting far
enough to bathe one end in undiluted sunshine. "Would
you like something to eat?" said Tourmaline.

"No, my stomach . . ." Vince started to say automatically, then reconsidered, realizing he was, indeed,
hungry. "Yes, please."

Tourmaline slid open a panel in the trunk and
extracted a bowl of fresh fruit. "What would you like
to drink?"

"Milk, please."

She obtained a tumbler from the same panel.

Looking around, she said, "Oh, I'm sorry," and a set of mushroomlike stools and table sprang up from the floor.

A small heap of peelings and fruit cores stacked quickly in front of Vince. "Do you live here all the time?"

Tourmaline shook her head. "I stay a number of places; but this is one of my favorites. I love to switch the screens off and sleep in the open on one of the upper platforms."

"This must cost a lot," said Vince. "Are you rich?"

Again she shook her head. "Only in the sense that considerable numbers of people enjoy my talents. The Network arranges these homes for me."

He looked at her inquiringly.

"My employer. It's basically an entertainment medium."

"You're in show business?"

"I'm an entertainer."

Vince finished the final orange.

"More?"

"I'd better not," he said wistfully.

She looked at him speculatively for a few seconds. "Would you like to go for a ride?"

"Where?"

"Over parts of Cinnabar."

"Why not." He spread his hands. "As long as I'm here I might as well see the sights. Can Mr. Obregon get in touch with us?"

"Call him Timnath. If he has anything to tell us, he can reach us." Tourmaline realized Vince was smiling for the first time since he had arrived in Cinnabar, as though it were only now that he had begun to enjoy the adventure.

"How will we go?" said Vince. "Not that—hallway; I've eaten too much."

"I've another vehicle," Tourmaline said. "It's perfect for sightseeing." She spread the remnants of Vince's meal out on the platform for the birds to pick. Then the two of them climbed stair after stair to the top of the tree.

When they emerged from the last branches of the crown, Vince sucked in his breath. "Wow!" He stared at the eighty-foot, cigar-shaped bag. "A balloon?"

"It's a helium blimp," said Tourmaline.

The metal stairs wound up around the pylon which served as a mooring tower. The blimp was painted bright blue, darker than the sky. About two-thirds of the way back along the stubby body of the gas bag, two pods with four-bladed propellers were suspended. Behind them were steering vanes.

"Where do we ride?" said Vince.

"There's a passenger platform ahead of the engines. It's transparent now."

"I'd rather have it opaque, I think."

They came up underneath the shadow of the airship and Tourmaline made a pass with her hand. The passenger platform opaqued—and it was just that: a platform with a single line around the perimeter as a safety railing. Vince cautiously climbed on and was surprised that the platform didn't rock.

"It's perfectly safe," said Tourmaline, following him.

Vince discovered that the platform was upholstered in a soft, comfortably deep pile. On his hands and knees, he carefully looked over the leading edge. The trees swayed below.

"Do you mind if I take this off?" said Tourmaline. "When I fly I don't like anything on my skin but the air and sun."

Vince said, "It's your dirigible."

"Blimp." She pulled the shift over her head and tossed it over the side. The dress fluttered down and hung like a blue pennant on one of the upper branches. "You ought to try this."

"I'm very comfortable," said Vince.

"You can look at me," said Tourmaline. "I'll be very upset if you continue to pretend there's a blind spot in your eye every time you look at my body."

Vince's face flushed again.

Tourmaline cast off the mooring line. The twin propellers began to revolve. With a gentle whir, the airship launched into the skies above Cinnabar.

Tourmaline waved her arm in a lazy circle. "This is basically all there is to the world: the desert, the greenbelt, the city, and the sea."

"Aren't there any other cities?" said Vince.

"Not that I know of. Maybe one. Can you see that?" She pointed out toward the tan waste of the desert; Vince sighted along her forearm.

"What is it, a road?"

"It's the remnant of an elevated train track. I've seen the near terminus. The rails are ancient and corroded."

"Where does it go?"

"I have no idea. I've heard stories that it eventually crosses the desert and leads to a city called Els. No one I know can remember ever having seen a train arrive from Els."

"Haven't you ever tried going there?"

"Never," said Tourmaline. "The desert makes me uncomfortable." She considered. "Perhaps some day, if I get bored enough, I'll try."

"I'd try it."

"You've enough to explore here in Cinnabar." She turned back toward the city and began to point out local sights: "The Tancarae Institute, Craterside Park, the Neontolorium, Serene Village—that's where the unredeemable elderly live, the Klein Expressway, the Balloon Works—"

"Where they made your blimp?"

She nodded. "There's the Natural History Club, that long, low building. And on beyond, if you shade your eyes, you can see the red bluffs; below them is Tondelaya Beach."

"What's that?" Vince pointed to an ovoid structure gleaming like a giant aluminum egg.

"That's a biogenesis center."

"I'm a zoo major." He added, "I haven't decided how I'm going to specialize, but I know I want to be a biologist."

"The center would probably interest you," she said. "Would you like to investigate?"

"Sure," said Vince. "Do they really create life

there? Where I came from, we're still trying to synthesize a virus."

"Virtually anything can be accomplished in a biogenesis center. They cater to all individual options."

"Even test-tube babies?" said Vince.

Tourmaline looked puzzled.

Vince struggled to recall the term. "Uh, ectogenesis. Growing a human embryo outside its mother's body."

Shocked, Tourmaline said, "How else?"

"You know—the natural way."

"In the mother's own womb?"

"Sure."

"That's disgusting," said Tourmaline. "Barbaric. It's Neo-Creelist dogma."

"Where I come from," said Vince, taken aback, "mothers have children."

"Not here," Tourmaline said. "Not if they have any sense."

"Were you—"

"I was decanted. So was my mother and my mother's mother."

"That's really spooky," said Vince.

"In fact, the only one of my friends I can ever recall actually bearing a child in their own body was Timnath."

It was Vince's turn to display puzzlement. "He's a man, isn't he?"

"Don't put stock in superficial genotypes. Somatics can be altered as well. Timnath went to the center and had a uterus implant performed. He carried the child for nearly a full term." She paused reflectively. "Timnath has a more curious bent than anyone else I know, but even he didn't want to carry it through. He had the foetus transferred to a host mother."

"A woman?"

"No, a cow."

Vince attempted to digest all this. "Are you kidding me?"

"Of course not."

"But a cow?"

"Animals are very loving mothers." She added soberly, "Since the biological freeing of the rest of us, I sometimes suspect animals have become the new oppressed class."

Vince said skeptically, "What about the maternal instinct?"

"There's no such thing."

"Well, there *was*."

"Let's be precise," said Tourmaline. "There is a biological basis for the sex drive and for the caring for the young of any species. As for a specific drive toward pregnancy—probably once there was one. But after technology liberated us, we acculturated it out of existence."

"You sound like one of my professors at D.U."

"I studied this when I did some Network propaganda shows. You see, not everybody's liberated—" She stopped as a rock arched over the platform, narrowly missing Vince's head.

The airship had descended toward the biogenesis center in a gentle spiral. Vince peered over the edge of the passenger platform. About thirty feet below, a dozen men and women dressed in somber clothing gesticulated upward angrily. Some threw more stones. Several carried placards:

> THERE'S ONLY ONE WAY—NATURALLY

"What's happening?" said Vince.

"Neo-Creelists. I don't think we'll be visiting the center today."

"Who are they?"

"They term themselves creative anachronists. They're misguided romantics trying to capture a past that never existed."

> MOTHERHOOD IS SACRED

Several of the women were visibly pregnant.

"They oppose ectogenesis as historically unnatural," said Tourmaline.

"Can't they have children as they want?"

"Of course."

"Then why are they throwing stones?"

"Having found their truth, they worry it like an animal with a bone. They want to force their sick nostalgia on the rest of us."

TWO SEXES! NO MORE, NO LESS!

A furious voice carried up to them: "Down with the heterogyne's whore!"

"They recognize me," said Tourmaline. "Another benefit of being a star."

"Heterogyne?"

"Timnath. They're offended by his bearing of his own child."

The voices grew fainter as the airship ascended above the surly crowd.

"We can try the center again tomorrow. The anachronists are likely to become bored and leave. They're more unpleasant than dangerous." She adjusted the airship's controls and then yawned, stretching her arms wide.

Vince watched her breasts rise with the motion and furiously willed himself not to blush, knowing he had no control over the blood rushing to his face. "Now where are we going?"

"I've parked us against the wind." A pair of gray gulls circled the platform curiously and then flew on. Tourmaline moved closer to Vince. "I'm slowly deducing things about your culture," she said. "As with the Neo-Creelists, I'm afraid I'm a little appalled."

"I'm sorry," Vince said automatically.

"There's nothing for you to be sorry for. What appalls me is the thought of a world in which biological options are so limited. It's hard for me to imagine a culture in which progeny are automatically equivalent with the pain and discomfort of mandatory childbirth. Have you ever thought of what it really must feel like to give birth?"

"No," said Vince.

"I suppose not. You're locked into your own role."

"But if you haven't had a baby," said Vince defensively, "how do you *know*?"

"I can extrapolate," said Tourmaline. "Besides that, I've experienced sensory recordings of childbearing. The Network runs them as part of their horror-show series." She took his hand. "You must think I'm quite a coward—well, I am. But it isn't just the pain. I've got a feeling that the months of discomfort would breed in me a vested interest in the child—as if it owed me something. I hate possessiveness." Guiding his fingers, she continued, "My cunt was never intended for that sort of abuse."

Vince tensed, but let himself touch her.

"The girl Karen," she said. "What did you want her to do with you?"

Vince thought. "I wanted her to like me."

Tourmaline laughed. "Be specific."

"To—kiss me."

"Is that all?"

"No."

"Tell me all the things."

He told her; and she did them.

The declining afternoon brought a chill to the shaded platform below the airship. Tourmaline stirred restlessly and woke Vince up. "It's getting cold now. Let's start back."

"I really feel relaxed," said Vince.

"You should." She fed power to the blimp's engines and took manual control of the steering vanes. "Would you like to stop by Timnath's and see how he's proceeding?"

"I thought the same thing," said Vince. "Sure." The airship began to drone across the sky. With seeming nonchalance, Vince put his hand on the pilot's upper thigh.

"All of a sudden you're a cauldron of energy," she said, laughing. "Were you really a virgin?"

He nodded and took his hand away.

"It's not an insult," she said. "I just have grave reservations about a culture that forces a sixteen-year-old to keep those tensions bottled up. It must be very uncomfortable."

"It's awful. You know, I used to sit in the dorm and listen to guys when they came in after a date, and sometimes I knew they were lying, but sometimes they were telling the truth. And even if I was really young, I used to wonder how long it would take for me, or even if I ever would. Then I'd try to study for an exam or something, but I'd finally give up and lock the door and go to bed; and then I'd—I'd beat off."

Tourmaline ilstened to the torrent sympathetically, trying to remember how it had been to be young. Her memories of the time were sketchy and approximate. She kissed him and let her head tuck into the juncture between his chin and neck.

"Look!" said Vince. "I can see the lab, and there's smoke—"

The laboratory was a two-storeyed white structure perched at the top of its hill. Dense black smoke poured from the lower floor. They could see human figures milling about outside.

"There must have been an accident," said Tourmaline. She touched the controls and the pitch of the propellers whined up the scale.

"It was the time machine," said Vince. "Maybe it blew up."

The airship angled lower toward the dark plume. One of the capering figures beside the burning lab looked into the sky and began to shout something indistinguishable. They were close enough to hear the crackling flames.

"Those aren't firemen."

"Damn them to hell," said Tourmaline. "They're Neo-Creelists." The airship's engines began to strain against the updraft of heat. The fire had the odor of overdone barbecue. "Timnath—"

Vince pointed. "He's on the roof!"

The swirling smoke parted for a moment and she saw Obregon waving his arms frantically. Below, the

Neo-Creelists set up a howl and began to hurl rocks and bottles. The airship settled ponderously toward the roof.

"Wow, it's like a movie," Vince said. "The good guys to the rescue."

Tourmaline said, "Don't be a romantic. The Neo-Creelists are romantics enough."

Obregon didn't wait for the airship to touch down. When the passenger platform was level with his head, he jumped and caught hold of the safety line. Vince and Tourmaline hauled him onto the platform. Gasping for breath, he hugged them. "Good timing," he said. "Get out of here."

The airship began to rise. "The updraft will compensate for the extra weight," said Tourmaline. "We'll get enough altitude; we'll easily make it back to the tree."

From the ground, shrill cries of chagrin trailed after them.

"Did the Neo-Creelists do that?"

Obregon nodded. "One of the most amazing things that's ever happened to me. I'd brought the lab back from klein space and had taken the time machine up to the second level. Meanwhile, the Neo-Creelists sneaked around and threw an incendiary into the downstairs—I suspect they devised a pressure bomb out of an aerosol can of liquid fuel. There's not much on the second level but storage space, so I climbed up to the roof. But I was getting worried; I was afraid I'd have to jump and take my chances reasoning with those people."

"Aren't there any police?" said Vince.

"If a district wants rules, it makes up its own. For instance, Craterside Park's big on law and order; but their jurisdiction doesn't extend this far. Besides, no one suspected that the Neo-Creelists were capable of violence."

Tourmaline told him about the mob besieging the biogenesis center.

"They're certainly getting restive," commented Obregon. "I'll be glad when this nostalgia craze ends."

"They wanted to kill you."

"That occurred to me. I might even have accepted, had I not wanted to be able to continue the time-travel experiments."

"The time machine!" Vince said.

Obregon said, "No problem. The buzzing was merely an internal alarm indicating that the fuel supply was exhausted."

"No, the fire—"

Obregon looked uncomfortable. "That was the unfortunate thing. By now the machine has almost certainly been destroyed."

"What'll happen?"

"I don't know."

"Am I stuck here?"

"That, also, I'm afraid I don't know."

"Your clothing stinks of smoke," Tourmaline said to the two of them. "Throw it over the side; we don't need the weight." Both obliged; Vince, hesitating momentarily.

The bright bits of fabric sailed down, disappearing into the dusk shadows before they hit the ground. Vince watched them fall and fade; he felt as lost.

On their level, the trunk of the tree rippled with a tawny firelight effect. Vince remembered the traditional Christmas tree he had never actually seen, but as his grandmother had described it: decorated with flickering candles attached to the live branches. He looked upward through the leafy canopy and could not tell where the candles stopped and the stars began.

Live grass carpeted the deck. To one side, the covering had been built up so that a shallow pool could be sunk. Water bubbled over the inboard lip from a concealed pump. The overflow cascaded off the deck in a thin sheet; long before reaching the forest floor, it dissipated into a fine mist.

Obregon sat between two lily pads, scrubbing his sooty arms. "I feel like I've been running races all day. Do you mind rubbing my back?"

"No," said Vince. He knelt on the bank behind Obregon.

"A little higher," Obregon directed.

"This morning," said Vince, "when you took the laboratory—away. Did you find out anything?"

"I've been debating whether to tell you. I discovered a number of things."

"I want to know."

Tourmaline descended the spiral stairs from the kitchen bower. Carrying a tray, she padded across the grass toward them. "I went to lengths with the soup," she said. "This is not a programed recipe."

"I'm ravenous," said Obregon. He splashed onto the bank like a clumsy otter.

The wooden bowls contained a thick stew of meat and vegetables. There were serving dishes filled with fruits and finger-sized loaves of dark bread and bundles of string cheese. A flagon brimmed with a clear, effervescent liquid. Tourmaline filled three tumblers.

Vince sipped cautiously and said, "It's like licorice ginger ale." He raised the glass to drink again, but Tourmaline put cautioning fingers on his wrist.

"Slowly . . . it's to be enjoyed."

"A toast!" said Obregon. Their glasses clinked dully together. "To you and your contemporary, Mr. Herbert George Wells."

"Really?" Tourmaline said to Vince, "I think that's exciting."

"H. G. Wells? He died before I was born."

"Close enough," said Obregon, "when you're considering all the recorded history of all recorded worlds. I took phrases like 'Denver University' and 'Central Texas College of Science' and your name and programed a wide-range, random association enquiry of Terminex."

"The computer?"

Obregon nodded smugly. "The results came from one of Terminex's most isolated random-information vaults. I discovered a six hundred and forty year 'gramed run of something called the *New York Times*."

"It was a newspaper—"

"Apparently a compilation of all trivial knowledge for an entire culture. But I found a number of references to you. I also discovered what may be a pertinent cross-reference to the Central Texas College of Science. It figured in the news on twenty-two November 1963, according to your calendar."

"That's today," said Vince.

"I found the reference in a small item on an interior page. It was the report of the deaths of two physicists in a small school in a province called Texas. Rather strangely, according to the reporter, the laboratory had imploded rather than exploded. An investigation was evidently launched, but I couldn't find any other references when I tracked ahead. In any case, the lone report was overshadowed by other news of the day."

"That must be where the time machine came from."

"At a guess, yes."

"But how did I get into this?"

"I very specifically checked, but there were no items about people mysteriously vanishing from a library in Denver."

"You said you found references to me."

"They were later."

"What kind of references?"

"Well," said Obregon uncomfortably. "One thing I read was your obituary."

Vince stared and started to say something, reconsidered, and then gulped a swallow of liquor.

"That's marvelous," said Tourmaline. "It means you must have returned to your own time." She looked at Obregon. "Isn't that right?"

"I'm cautious when trying to sort out temporal paradoxes."

"Stuff your paradoxes and tell me."

Obregon sighed. "If I can in fact believe the record of the *Times,* Vince did return to his own continuum."

Vince shook his head dazedly. "My obituary? When—"

"It would be unkind to tell you exactly," said Obregon. "But it was substantially later than when you evidently came here."

"My obituary," Vince repeated. "Then I'm dead."

"No," said Obregon. "You will be. That's an important distinction."

"You've got no concept of comfort," Tourmaline said to Obregon.

"I'm okay." Vince raised his glass shakily. "Why didn't you tell me before?"

"Bumbling though I am," said Obregon, "I'm still trying to avoid overloading your mind with shocks."

Tourmaline said, "I think Vince is a much stronger person than we guessed."

Vince sipped his drink. "This is like a roller coaster. The first few hills were scary, but now I guess I'm getting used to it."

"I don't know if it's any comfort, but I'm coming to suspect that the destroyed time machine is immaterial to your return to your own world."

"Did you check time travel in the *Times*?"

"Yes. There was nothing in reference to you."

"I'm not famous for being the first time traveler?"

"No, not for that."

"Something else?"

Obregon smiled. "That's a surprise I'll leave for you to discover."

The candle effects guttered and began to die. A night breeze stirred ripples on the pond.

Tourmaline yawned. "Come to bed."

"Where?" said Obregon.

"The platform with the furs. The night's turning cool."

"The three of us? Or two?"

Vince stared bewilderedly between the two of them.

"Oh," said Tourmaline. "So I'm the one forgetting cultural differences." She thought for a moment. "Two and one now. Maybe three later?"

Obregon nodded. "That kind of comfort will develop."

"Are you guys talking about, uh, sleeping arrangements?" Vince said.

"Yes. For tonight."

"I can sleep anywhere."

"Tonight," said Tourmaline, sounding maternal, "you'll sleep with me."

The soft, thick furs could be pulled over his face for a feeling of warm security; yet it was not stuffy beneath. The low-velocity component of the night wind circulated through the material. Vince cuddled against Tourmaline's body, wondering fleetingly why he hadn't noticed before that she was taller than he.

"I love you."

"You're such a strange mixture of adolescent and adult," she said. "I feel like I'm eating a pie and not knowing what fruit or spice is going to touch my tongue next."

"I do love you."

Tourmaline laughed softly in the darkness. "All the lovers I've had, and none has ever tempted me to become a mother."

"I don't understand."

"I suspect it's the drive I mentioned this afternoon—the one to care for the young of the species."

"Me?"

"Listen," she said. "Don't you know—you're a child I can love." She moved against him, lifting her leg across his body so that his own leg was held tight between her thighs.

"When I said I loved you, I—"

"Hush," she said. "No more of your romance. Love me tangibly."

Later, before they slept, Vince said, "You've done this with lots of men, haven't you?"

"Naturally," said Tourmaline. "And not just men."

He absorbed this information. "I must be really square."

"What does that mean?"

"I'm just not used to all this. Earlier, when you and Timnath were talking about who all were going to bed—was Timnath talking about sex?"

"Partially."

"The three of us together? I mean, having sex?"

"If it were mutually agreed to. Yes."

She felt his head shake slightly from side to side. "Back home—I mean in 1963—that's a perversion. It's against the law."

"You're not home," said Tourmaline reasonably.

"It's what I've been taught."

"You've been taught unbelievable strictures."

"I thought I really questioned things. But not until I got here—this is so wide open. It reminds me of reading about Utopias."

"Cinnabar? It's no Utopia. There are more options here than you've had before. That's all. There's diversity on an asymptotic curve that never quite touches total breakdown."

"Everything . . ." said Vince "A heterogyne having his own baby, the ectogenesis center, you, Timnath. I've never seen so much freedom."

Tourmaline's breathing became regular.

"Tourmaline?"

"What."

"I didn't mean to wake you up."

She rested on her elbows. "You started to ask me something."

"I really like Timnath." His voice stumbled. "If— he wants to sleep with us, I don't mind."

"Tomorrow."

"Okay. I mean, I'll try it."

"Fine."

Silence, for a minute.

"Tourmaline?"

"What." She sighed and sat up.

"Has there ever been anything in Cinnabar you couldn't have?"

Tempted to say "sleep," she said instead, "Only boredom."

"Really?"

"I apologize. I'm tired and I was being glib."

"If you really wanted, couldn't you have a child?"

"I suppose. If I really wanted; but I don't. Why are you so persistent?"

"I'm curious," said Vince.

"You know why I won't bear a child. I doubt I'll

ever clone an offspring or use any other ectogenetic technique."

"You like to mother," said Vince, "without actually being one."

She considered that. "It's a harmless indulgence. I'm justifiably and unashamedly selfish."

"One thing we learned was that perpetuating the species is a biological truth."

"We learned, we learned," she mocked. "You know so damned much theory."

"Shut up!" He pressed her shoulders down against the furs. "You treat me like—"

"—a child."

"Well, I'm not."

"But you're close." She kissed him. "And you're tired."

He subsided. "I am."

She drew him near and sang soft songs. He fell asleep a few seconds before she did.

In his dream, Vince consummated a quest.

The journey not being easy, Vince was obliged to climb a rocky pinnacle. The mountain rose from the otherwise smooth surface of a tan and desolate plain. Vince was acutely aware of textures. The rock faces he scaled, the ledges he traversed, the steep chimneys he negotiated, did not feel like stone. Surfaces, as soft and resilient as flesh buttressed with bone, sank with his steps. Clambering up an uneven slope that reminded him of a field of shoulder blades, he lost his footing and almost fell. He cried out; his voice, peculiarly muffled, did not echo.

"Where are you?"

Nothing and no one answered him.

"Where are you?"

He stopped confused because he could not recall whom he was calling.

The air chilled and thickened with a hum. *Keep climbing,* said a voice. Vince stared up the mountainscape but saw no one. *Keep climbing.* He continued to struggle upward.

"Just a little farther." Still no one visible. The voice was a pleasant soprano. "Here I am."

Vince realized he had conquered the peak and there was nowhere more to climb. The summit consisted of a flat, clear area roughly the size and shape of a basketball court. A being appeared.

It took the form of a golden double helix, whose spirals danced and burned with burnished flames. "It's about time."

"It's a tall mountain," said Vince.

"Well, it can't be helped," said the double helix. "Dream quests are noted for their arduousness."

Vince said, "Are you God?"

"Of course not," said the being. "I'm surprised at you."

"Then what are you?"

"Consider me something basic and something utterly human. How arrogant that you think me God."

"Well," said Vince, "I can see that you aren't an old man on a throne ordering the universe."

The double helix said, "It was wrong of you to anthropomorphize."

Vince studied his own toes.

"No matter. I expect you're wondering why I had you climb up here."

Vince looked up; the shimmering strands seemed to tug at his eyes.

"I've something to give you, to take back to the people." A flaming strand of RNA messenger darted out and began to inscribe on the mountaintop between them. The ground trembled as though in torment.

Vince stared at the fiery letters. "I can't read it."

"It is the greatest of my commandments. Remember this. Biologically speaking," said the double helix, "there are no imperatives." The incised letters arranged themselves: NO IMPERATIVES.

"But there *are*," said Vince. "We learned—"

"Are you arguing with life?" said the double helix.

"But—"

"Take my word to the people." The fiery strand withdrew and was rewound by its parent spiral. "Pick it up."

The fire had burned a border around NO IM-
PERATIVES so as to form a rectangular tablet. Vince
bent and picked it up. The stone was soft and the same
temperature as his skin. He gripped the tablet tightly
and felt a pulse beating within it.

"Go."

For a sacrilegious moment he wished to defy the
double helix. Then he turned without a word and began to descend the mountain.

The helix called after him, "Beware the barbarians."

As on cue, the hordes of uncouth barbarians
arose from their hiding places among the rocks. They
charged up the slope toward him, screaming and rat-
tling their weapons. Their shrill cries filled up his ears
as though with blood.

"Vince! There are men—they want to kill us."

"Mmh? Dream . . . Lemme sleep." Submerged in
the furs, he drifted in and out of the dream.

"Vince, wake up." She shook him urgently. Then
she cried out in pain and fell away from him.

He jerked awake, still hearing the cries of the
barbarians. "Tourmaline—"

She crawled back into his field of vision, face
bloody, holding a jagged piece of stone half the size
of her fist. "They hurt me," she said wonderingly. She
leaned over Vince, staring. Blood dripped from her
nose to his cheek. "They'll kill us."

"And well you deserve it," said an angry voice.

Vince turned and saw three men standing on the
edge of the sleeping platform. All wore the dull blacks
of the Neo-Creelists. Each was armed: the first clutched
a metal bludgeon, the second held a stiletto with a long
blade like a needle, and the third had a pouch filled
with stones slung from his waist. The third man looked
disgusted and tossed a desultory stone. It struck Tourmaline in the shoulder; she recoiled, but did not cry
out.

It was the man with the knife who had spoken.
"You must know this is not a personal thing," he said.

The assassin with the bludgeon said, "I always

used to catch your shows. I thought you were great."

The man with the stones looked even more sour. "Can't we get this over with?"

"You're all insane," said Tourmaline. She touched her fingers to the cut above her eye and then inspected the blood. Vince scrambled to his feet.

"It was those filthy propaganda shows you did for the Network," said the stiletto man.

"Did they harm you?" said Tourmaline.

"Not me. I was already sure of the truth. But I can imagine the effect on more impressionable people."

"I was only trying to educate—"

"To evil," said the stiletto man. "Against nature."

"Nature is healthy when it's diverse. That's all I—"

"Trash," said the bludgeon man. "Sick, perverted trash."

The three assassins moved apart from one another as they advanced slowly across the platform.

Vince cursed his nakedness. "Get behind me," he said to Tourmaline. He tried to push her back to what small safety he could offer.

"You're insane too," she said. "This is not a historical romance; you can't save me."

"I can try." He stepped in front of her.

"Please," she said to the assassins. "Don't do this. I haven't interfered with your lives."

The stiletto man said, "You've gone against the truth. That's sufficient."

The man with the stones said, "Some of the women are grumbling."

"Don't kill the boy," said Tourmaline.

"I expect he's tainted," said the stiletto man, as though that settled the issue. "Now let us finish this."

Vince grabbed up one of the rugs at his feet and threw it over the stiletto man. Arms windmilling, the assassin reeled back. Vince leaped at the bludgeon man on his right. The man held his club before him in a clumsy defense; Vince felt his fist sink into the man's solar plexus. He knew amazement; never before had he fought. He brought back his fist again, but someone grabbed him from behind—the man with the pouch of stones. Wiry arms wrapped around his chest, pinning his arms.

The bludgeon man attempted to straighten up; his breath ratcheted in his throat. He raised his head and looked hatefully at Vince.

"Lousy cloned bastard!" Vince recognized the voice of the stiletto man behind him. "This for you, motherless scum."

Vince felt a prick low in his left side; a small cold pain like the stab of a hypodermic needle. He tried to wrench free, but succeeded only in overbalancing his captor and they both toppled to the soft floor. Then he heard low wounded-animal cries and realized after a seeming eternity that they were his.

Another cry in the background—Tourmaline. Again he attempted to free himself, but he had no strength. He tried to yell and there was no sound.

Am I dying? he thought. *It doesn't hurt.*

But soon enough it did, and that is when the darkness bore him away in a soft rush of silence.

This time there was no bright dream; only the feel of textures. His boyhood fever fantasies replayed: a tactility both smooth and sticky. Things slid across his skin, yet simultaneously clung. The paradox stirred a core of nausea. The moment stretched . . .

He awoke into a gentle white light. Vince opened his eyes and discovered he was lying recumbent, naked, on a cushioned table. The man standing over him had a familiar face. "Timnath?"

The man shook his head. "Gerald. I'm his son." He wore a pale green smock.

"Are you a doctor?"

"That, too. I'm a healer."

"What happened?"

"You want a catalogue?" Gerald ticked off the items on his fingers: "Two skewered kidneys, complete renal failure, massive shock, a torn aorta, a punctured inferior vena cava. Those are the major items. Would the complete list interest you?"

"No, I don't think so." Vince closed his eyes.

"What amazes me," said Gerald, "is that all your wounds came from a thrust and twist of that meat-skewer of a knife."

"Those men! Where's Tourmaline?"

"Here, of course."

Vince opened his eyes and saw Tourmaline bending down to kiss him. She wore a black choker. "Really, you're all right?"

"Look for yourself." She pirouetted. There was no bruise on her shoulder, no scar above her eye.

"How long have I been asleep?"

"Three days," Gerald said. "You required some effort."

Vince moved his arms experimentally.

"Go ahead. You can sit up."

He did so gingerly. "I can really move like this three days after getting stabbed?"

Behind him, Timnath entered the room. "Remember the *New York Times?* You'll live to fill your obituary yet."

Vince swung his legs down off the table and sat on the edge. "Timnath, you're all right too?"

Tourmaline said, "He's fine; who do you think wandered down from his own sleeping platform and tossed those three assassins off ours?"

"I didn't mean to be quite so extreme," said Obregon. "It was reflex action, and I had the element of surprise."

"The tree needs the compost," said Tourmaline.

Vince said, "I was mostly asleep; I don't remember much. How'd they get up there?"

"Climbed," said Obregon. "Ropes, hooks, bark pitons. I found their gear on the lower porch."

"I've installed some precautions." She smiled grimly.

"Will there be more trouble?"

"I don't know," said Obregon. "I'm afraid they'll continue with their historical fantasies."

"As long as they keep their fantasies exactly that," said Tourmaline.

"Incidentally," said Obregon to Vince. "I've used the last three days to advantage in my temporal researches. My colleagues at Tancarae graciously helped outfit a new laboratory."

"What happened? Have you rebuilt the time machine?"

"No, I recovered your old machine from the remains of my former laboratory. I'm afraid that all that was left was a fused mass of glass and metal. A pity." He shook his head. "No, I've spent my time reasoning out a likely hypothesis for your return to your own time."

"Are you going to build a new machine?"

"I probably could, but I won't. There's a simpler and safer method for your return. In temporal mechanics there are specialized laws of matter and energy conservation. The physical fact that you and the machine are here in Cinnabar and not in 1963 creates a sort of gap in your proper continuum.

"When the machine brought you here, its self-contained power source provided the energy to maintain the time transfer. The residual effect kept you here after the machine was incapacitated in the fire, so your presence now is an indeterminate condition. There is a faint trail of dissipating energy leading from Cinnabar back to 1963. I call it a T-line. When the residual effect from the time machine can no longer stably maintain you here, you'll be pulled back along the T-line to your origin. Like nature, time abhors a vacuum."

"How long?" Tourmaline and Vince echoed each other.

Obregon said, "I don't know. If theory's correct, it could be anytime."

"Do I have to go back?" said Vince soberly. "Isn't there any way to stabilize me here?"

"I could apply energy indefinitely to keep the T-line open," said Obregon. "But I run into the problem of temporal paradoxes. You have a destiny back in your own continuum. I doubt it would be wise, attempting to fool with that."

"Bitchin'," said Vince.

"What?"

"Nothing. I just realized how much I've been trying to forget 1963."

Tourmaline put her arms around his shoulders and held him tightly.

Gerald Obregon produced a tray of instruments. "Temporal mechanics is fascinating, but there are a few more tests before I can let this person go."

Vince saw a sheen of tears in Tourmaline's eyes. She said, "We'll wait for you outside in the park." She turned and Obregon and she left.

"You owe her quite a lot," said Gerald, lightly touching Vince's abdomen with a cold silver rod.

"I know."

"You don't." Gerald poked hard enough to make him wince. "You didn't listen when I told you you'd suffered total renal failure. She gave you one of her kidneys. Not that it's anything momentous, but it's a very nice gesture."

Vince swallowed dryly, without saying anything.

"The organ is gerontologically stable," continued Gerald. "It should certainly function longer than your own body. My father told me about your culture."

"We've had kidney transplants in 1963," said Vince, "but they don't work if they're not between blood relatives. There's a natural rejection syndrome."

Nonplused, Gerald said, "I've already ensured that your body will accommodate the kidney with a temporary over-supply of one-handed antibodies. Your body cannot recognize the new organ as foreign. There will be no problem with either two-handed antibodies or blood complement."

Vince looked thoughtful. "You heard what Timnath said about the T-line and my returning to my own time. Even if the kidney's in me, isn't it still Tourmaline's tissue and doesn't it belong here in Cinnabar? It's going to be rough on me if it vanishes and comes back here along its own T-line."

"Timnath thought of everything." Pride tinged Gerald's voice. "He gave me a subminiature energy supply to implant in the kidney; it's only about as large as a few thousand nephrons; you'll never notice. It will last as long as the kidney."

"I'm a cyborg," said Vince.

"So? There's no social stigma."

"That was sort of a joke."

"Mmph." Gerald made a few concluding prods and replaced the rod on the tray. "I'd say you're quite ready. You can even drink all the liquids you wish."

Vince climbed off the table carefully, finding that his legs were weak.

"Get some exercise." Gerald smiled for the first time. "Enjoy your stay."

With some modification of the frame and skin, and the addition of another helium compartment for increased lift, Tourmaline's airship accommodated three easily. The wind thrummed between the struts supporting the engine pods and brought the salt smell from the ocean. Gulls curiously orbited the craft. Momentarily cold, the three passengers drew around them one of the broad furs borrowed from the sleeping platform.

"What will it be like?" said Vince.

"Sudden," Obregon said. "No suspenseful blurring in and out of reality, with a final slow fade. Very neat and clean."

"That's a relief."

The airship sailed on toward the red bluffs overshadowing Tondelaya Beach. The gulls, bored, veered back toward the sea.

"My time here's been good," said Vince. He sat between Tourmaline and Obregon. Their arms were around his shoulders. "I know that's a dumb way to say it, but I wanted to try and say how I feel."

"You sound like you're saying good-bye," said Tourmaline. "You don't know that it's time yet."

"I feel like it is."

All three sat silently for a while, watching Cinnabar's towers glide by beneath.

"I've really come to love both of you," said Vince.

"I think the feeling's reciprocated," Obregon said.

"Whatever happens when I get home, I won't forget all this."

Tourmaline, smiling, laid a slender finger across his lips.

"I won't," he repeated. "I can't."

The airship cleared the bluffs and they saw the sand and the steady slow waves.

Vince said, "I don't want to leave. You know, I never—"

He vanished. Air rushed together, filling the space where he had been with an audible *plock*.

"I imagine," said Obregon, "that those kilos of slagged time machine in my laboratory have also plocked out of existence." He wiped tears from his face.

Tourmaline looked away, down toward the clean sand. She said, "I feel very sad."

"—this morning in Dallas," said the radio.

In varying degrees of shock, students and library personnel gathered around the desk.

"—apparently fired from an upper floor of the Texas Book Depository. At this time, no one—"

A whisper of disturbed air swirled behind them. No one noticed.

Vince Blake stumbled forward, fingers pressed against the cold metal reality of the bar of the revolving door. Disoriented, he emerged into the open air where two coeds, climbing the steps, giggled at his dazed look.

He shook his head and decided that today was one day he could afford to cut his zoology quiz. That evening he returned to the library to research the current state of immunology in regard to the rejection problems of organ transplants.

"Do you suppose he's all right?" said Tourmaline. Obregon said, "I know he is."

They lay in a striped red-and-blue hammock strung between two of the topmost boughs in Tourmaline's tree. It was a place to listen to the busy insect noises in the leaves around them. The afternoon sun burned their skins a richer brown.

Tourmaline trailed her fingernails down Obregon's chest. "Will you tell me now about his obituary?"

"It wouldn't depress you?"

She shook her head.

Obregon said, "He won a Nobel Prize."

"Is that good?"

"Apparently the best of his time. It was awarded for his achievements in genetics and human reproductive biology."

"Then he remained in the life sciences as his chosen field. That's good."

Obregon nodded. "He became known as the so-called father of the biological revolution, a title that evidently afforded him great amusement. It was an odd achievement to gain that distinction. He was a strong individualist in a time noted for team approaches to scientific research."

"Did he remain unmarried?"

"Yes. Why?"

She laughed. "I was afraid I'd find out that he had lived a long and monogamous life with someone named Karen."

"He was mourned by his own descendants."

"That's good."

Obregon paused. "Vince was also reviled by most of his own generation. In the last years of his life he was popularly termed a traitor to his species."

"Tell me," said Tourmaline.

"Vince pioneered in ectogenesis."

Tourmaline slowly began to smile.

"He had a flare for the propaganda value of public exposure. When he entered his maturity, he bore a child. The cultural impact was incalculable; he was the first woman-alternate, the first heterogyne."

"Magnificent," said Tourmaline.

"There's more. Receiving the first rejectionless implant of a uterus was only half the experiment. The other half was the embryo's origin; it was cloned from Vince's own body tissue."

Her eyes widened and she opened her mouth to speak.

"The tissue came from his kidney. He named his daughter Tourmaline."

Tourmaline was speechless.

"One could say that at long last you're a mother," said Obregon.

"And a father."

He said, "And that."

"Is there a happy ending?"

"I hesitate to tell you," said Obregon. "He was assassinated by persons unknown. His martyrdom aided the movement his supporters founded."

She stared away toward the trees below. "Was he old, by then?"

"He was old."

"I don't know whether to laugh or cry."

"Whichever," he said. "It was a good ending."

"Then I'll smile," said Tourmaline.

Their bodies touched and, for a moment, they were three together. Then only two again, and the two wept because they felt the loss.

6

Years
Later

*Arthur Sand on brutality: "The older I
get, the less subtlety I can handle."*

There once was a time when a few people in Cinnabar
aged relatively quickly. As a refuge for these elderly,
Terminex established Serene Village. The village was
located about halfway between City Center and the
greenbelt, just above the north beach. Serene Village
was a collection of winding paths, simulated woods,
rustic cottages, and blue ponds.

Most inhabitants of Serene Village lived alone.
They were among the few in Cinnabar resistant to
anti-agathics. Radiation, medication, and spectrum sur-
gery were only palliatives. Gland transplants from the
sea snark were useless. These people grew wilted and
wrinkled like old lettuce.

Arthur Sand lived in a large cottage near the upper point of one of the most beautiful ponds. With him
were his wife Estrella and daughter Leah. Though nuclear families in the village were rare, Leah had wanted
to remain with her parents. She appealed to Network
and, as Leah was a promising young director, Network
relayed the request up to Terminex. The computer,
for its own reasons, assented.

Years passed and Leah Sand was troubled. She
realized that she had never seen her parents fight. Too,

she did not understand her father's behavior. Arthur had his fantasy workshop to keep him occupied and happy, and his fantasies-in-life grew steadily more brutal.

One day Leah made an attempt to talk with a psychosocial counselor. "It's my parents. When we still lived outside the village, everyone talked about the principle of periodicity. They said it was the only way people could grow older without wanting to kill each other. I don't mind staying with my parents, but they've accompanied each other for two centuries straight. Father must feel the strain."

The counselor, a resurrectronic bust of Freud, nodded sagely. "It's a responsibility. Try not to worry."

"There's a rehearsal." She felt she couldn't trust a counselor made of metal.

Arthur Sand surveyed the spread-eagled body of his wife. She was nailed at feet and hands with spikes. "Please, Arthur, it hurts so much."

"And so it should, dear. I specified that the spikes be blunt and rusty."

Arthur bent down and tapped the nail piercing her right foot. She arched her back, then lay flat against the plank floor. "This tires me," he said. Arthur set a rack of bottles on the floor and unwrapped a selection of spun-glass brushes.

Estrella turned her head.

"I'm going to paint a beach scene, love." He dipped a brush and began to swab liquid on her bare midriff. Finally he sat back on his heels, satisfied. "It's a perfect seascape." He checked his watch and silently counted off the seconds.

"Now!" The timed selective acids began to react and foam, eating into the topography of Estrella's abdomen. "Quickly," he said. "Look at your belly."

The acids fed at different rates. Estrella stared down her body and briefly saw a crude relief map of Cinnabar. Then she closed her eyes as her dissolving aorta let a bloody tide wash across the city.

"Beautiful," said Arthur. He watched his artwork

subside into a pulsing tidal pool. He thought vaguely of masturbating and felt a sudden, bitter loss.

When Leah returned home to Serene Village for supper, she found her mother seated outside the cottage in the sun. The pond reflected an oblique view of Estrella's latest tapestry. It was an unfinished portrait of Nekhbet the vulture goddess. Estrella looked up and smiled at her daughter.

"Where's Father?" Leah asked.

"I expect he's in his workshop."

Mother and daughter appraised each other. They looked enough alike to be mistaken for twins. Only Estrella's eyes betrayed her age; gray, but pale as though bleached by time.

"Do you love Father?"

"That's an odd word, Leah. Love is a transient cultural concept. It came back into vogue shortly before you were born."

"But do you love him?" Leah persisted.

"Not often. I occasionally like him. I am intermittently loyal."

"That's unfair to you. You kept our family nuclear."

"I grew accustomed," she said bitterly. "I am more a person of habit than most." She looked down at the warping frame. "I know him too well. Your father and I have lived together for nearly two hundred years. We haven't touched more intimately than brushing past each other in the hallway for almost one hundred of those years."

"Mother—"

"He's *old*," she said. "He's dying. Someday I may die. Perhaps, eventually, even you. But Arthur's rotting while we watch."

"Then why have you stayed?"

Her mother looked back at her steadily. "It would be immoral to leave him to die here alone. I cannot abandon him as these others in the village have been left."

Leah put her hand on her mother's shoulder. Estrella covered it with her own. "He's slower this year than last," Leah said. "I wish—"

"There is nothing."

Leah said, "Perhaps cryonics . . ."

"He won't agree to preservation. For him, cryonics is death. He would have to be forced."

"Only criminals can be forced."

"And your father is a good man." Leah nearly missed the irony.

"It isn't fair."

"You should leave," said Estrella. "I can manage Arthur while he plays in his workshop with those stupid, cruel charades. I will watch your father die."

"I've thought about leaving."

Shadows lengthened over the pond. "We should fix supper," Estrella said. "Help me."

Estrella Sand was manacled to the table. Her flesh puffed tightly around the edges of the metal cuffs.

"Hungry, dear?" Arthur slapped her belly with the flat of a spatula.

She twisted her neck to look at him. "No."

"Well, you're not eating anyway."

"What are you going to do?"

"Nothing. My little friends will do it." He tightened a band around his wife's head. With a metal pick, he pried open her jaws and inserted the narrow mouth of a funnel. Carefully remaining within her vision, Arthur opened a black case and shook several objects into his palm. He took one between thumb and forefinger. "You know what this is?"

Her eyes widened.

Arthur rolled the silver sphere between his fingers. "Correct. A common kitchen helper—but with a difference. It's been programed to eat something more exotic than dust or pencil shavings. Imagine them tunneling down through your body until they reach your ovaries."

Estrella screamed.

Arthur smiled and emptied his palm into the funnel. The kitchen helpers dropped into Estrella's wet mouth. Arthur watched with clinical attention.

"Do you remember the meals we used to fix on the beach? Remember how I inevitably would burn myself starting the fire? We would eat and then make love beside the surf."

His eyes filmed over with tears as he pulled up her dress and gently drew her legs apart.

A bay window, overlooking the pond, fronted the dining room. From their table, the Sands could watch the sunset through diamond-shaped panes. Silently they passed around the platter of soybland steaks. Leah disliked soybland, but ate it because it suited the taste of her father.

Between bites, Arthur said, "Leah, who's your immediate superior at Network?"

"His name's Liang."

"In programing, isn't he?"

Leah nodded.

"I was wondering . . ."

She looked down at her plate. She had heard the gambit before.

"What are the chances that maybe you could take me in for an audition?"

"Arthur," Estrella said warningly.

Leah extemporized. "I don't think so, Father. All the shows are set for next season. There won't be any auditions for quite a while."

Her father chewed ruminatively. "Well, I just thought it was about time I got off my rear and did something useful." He smiled. "Wouldn't you like to see me in a comeback?"

"That would be lovely, Father." Leah pretended to drop her napkin so she could lean down and wipe her eyes. Arthur had once been the foremost cynocist at the Center for Morbid Culture.

"Something spectacular," said Arthur. "Lots of visuals." His wife passed him a plate of bread. "An arena show. Network hasn't done an arena show in a long time, has it?"

"No, Father."

"They neglect the classics," said Arthur. His voice grew more excited. "Programs today are too sophisticated. We can get back to basics. Next season . . ." He reached across the table to clasp his wife's hand.

"Foolishness," said Estrella. She withdrew her hand.

The three stared at each other; outside, the pond turned black.

In the morning, a message from Network waited for Leah when she entered her office. She scanned the paper: "TALK TO ME—LIANG."

She found Liang on the ninety-ninth floor of the Black Tower, administrative headquarters for all Network. Liang sat cross-legged in the center of a spacious, gray-tiled chamber. He was using a touch-controlled panel to deform holographic projections. He motioned when he saw Leah.

Leah approached him. Liang looked up from ancient eyes set in a smooth, youthful face. "Don't tower," he said.

The girl folded her legs and sat facing him. "It's not about my documentaries, is it?"

"Your work is fine," said Liang. "I think that soon you will be given a larger crew and the chance for something more challenging."

"That's the sweetener. There's something else."

Liang nodded. "Forgive me for not coming immediately to the point."

"Which is?"

"Budget has sent me a memo. They think our requisition of simulacrae somewhat excessive."

"It was part of the agreement when I joined Network . . ."

"Your father's demands have increased over the years," said Liang. "Simulacrae are valuable and the supply not inexhaustible."

Leah said, "Perhaps just not so often . . ."

"There are budget cuts all over. I'm afraid everything will have to stop."

Leah looked at her superior pleadingly.

"Truly, I regret this."

She stood and backed away.

"Wait," said Liang. "Don't you want to know what you will be making next?"

Leah shook her head and turned toward the exit. "Drama."

"Father," Leah said. "Will you brush my hair?"

Arthur looked up from his Bosch folio. "Of course." He put the volume down and the tiny scenes vanished.

"Let's go into the living room."

They sat on a low couch and Leah angled her back toward her father. "Do you mind?"

"Of course not. I love your hair." He stroked the long, ebony length of it before taking the brush. "How long have I done this?"

"Fifty years. Perhaps sixty. One of the first things I remember is you holding and rocking me, and stroking my hair."

"I remember," said Arthur. "It was the year I headlined the inquisition troupe at the Center."

Silence passed while the brush hissed through Leah's hair.

"Father, I want to talk to you."

"Don't we ever talk?"

"Not enough. I'm being serious."

"You were always serious." He laughed. "Go ahead. What is it?"

Bristles scraped the back of her neck; Leah felt her muscles tighten. "Have you thought lately about cryonics?"

"The freezer?" Arthur's cadenced strokes didn't falter. "Not a chance. I won't see myself stored away like a few kilos of steak. It's undignified. Besides, I don't trust doctors. I suspect nothing would ever develop to warrant awakening me." He set the brush down slowly. "I don't want to be trapped between life and death. I'll take the first one up to the point of the second, and then welcome the second. But not a compromise."

"Father . . ."

"Do I cause any trouble, Leah? Do I moan and

wail in self-pity? Look at me. In this city, even in this insane era, I'm a genetic freak. When I'm only bones, you'll still be young."

"The freezer—"

"No! The gene codes will always be twisted the wrong way. I'm dying. Hell, I'm dead."

Leah hugged her father; his arms tightened convulsively around her. "I'm sorry, baby," he said, stroking her hair again.

"I'm sorry too. I didn't want to upset you."

"What is it, Leah? Is it something about your mother and me?"

Leah looked away. "I talked to Mother last night. Do you hate each other?"

Arthur's smile was hard and brief. "Sometimes we do. It's wrong, of course. I should have sent her away long ago. We both should have made you leave. That's what periodicity's all about. People can get together again when they've forgotten a bit about what one another was like. I take the blame. I'm old and not always lucid; and worse, I'm weak."

Finally, Leah said, "Liang called me in this morning."

"Oh?"

Leah faltered. "I'm going to be promoted to drama," she said miserably.

"Why, that's good news," her father said. "Fine news, indeed."

Leah found her mother outside the cottage, standing under the trees. Together they contemplated the darkness.

"This morning, Liang told me that no more simulacrae will be delivered."

"Have you told him?"

"I tried. I couldn't."

"Do they expect him to play at card tricks the rest of his days?" Estrella said bitterly.

"I wish I knew Father better. You and Father."

"You will," said Estrella. "You'll have your first man or woman, and then you'll begin to know. The longer the relationship lasts, the more you'll accumulate the infinite bits of information about someone else. Your lover will learn the same things about you."

"I think I'd like that."

"A philosopher once said that love is novelty and hate is knowledge. It's difficult to balance on the blade between; too easy to slip."

Daughter reached out to mother in the darkness. "What will we do?"

"I don't know what I will do. You should leave."

"I can't. Not until Father—dies."

She found Liang still in his room of gray tile, still surrounded by phantom polyhedrons.

Liang looked up and motioned her into the room. "You have some problem?"

"Is there no chance of Budget changing its mind?"

He shook silky hair back from his eyes. "Not a chance, Leah."

"Surely there's some appeal?"

"Not on budgetary matters. Perhaps next season."

"That's stupid."

"That's Terminex, ultimately. Terminex knows our resources and budgets accordingly."

"I could quit."

"That would be silly," said Liang.

"But what can I do?"

"I've read the file. It's foolish for nuclear families to attempt such longevity. Have your father volunteer for the cryonics vault."

"He won't do it."

Liang shrugged. "Then he will have to accommodate. People always do."

"Today's the last delivery?" Leah asked.

Liang shook his head. "Yesterday morning."

"Yesterday?" Shocked, Leah pressed her fist against her mouth. "It can't—"

Liang nodded, face somber. Leah stared at him a moment, before turning silently and rushing to the door. Liang watched as she disappeared; then snapped his fingers and was surrounded by a dozen clean, sleek tetrahedrals.

Arthur locked the door of his den. "I'm in a good mood," he said.

His wife looked back at him with no trace of emotion.

Arthur hefted the ax so its blade glittered in the light. "Cold, sharp, and clean," he said. He moved closer to Estrella. "I'm sorry. No antishock medicine this time. It would dilute the cleanness of the act." He swung the ax back over his shoulder.

Something flickered in Estrella's eyes. She stepped aside and the blade crashed down among shelved souvenirs. Arthur staggered forward and almost fell. Looking at Estrella crouched in the corner, he whispered, "It must be clean." He swung his arm and again brought down the ax.

The blade split her skull evenly along the line of her nose. Straddling her waist, he continued to chop, separating arms and legs at the major joints.

He picked up her limbless torso and laid it on the table; then began to disrobe. "I loved you," he said.

Leah left the Klein Expressway at the first exit for Serene Village. A few elderly inhabitants watched curiously from their sunny benches. She ran across the winding trails, through the woods, past the rustic cottages. Rounding the tip of the pond, she took the steps of the path two at a time.

Inside the house, Leah stopped. Her father sat in the living room. She slowly walked to the couch and sat beside him. She took his head in her lap and gently rocked back and forth.

7

Sharking
Down

The rough bluffs of reddish oxide awe the tourists venturing out of Cinnabar to view the sea. The visitors generally stand safely back from the long, crumbling escarpments, while below thunder the waves. There seems a sense of eternity in the measured surf which awes if not frightens a sufficient number of visitors so that most never essay a descent of the bluffs.

A few do climb down to the beach. They doff their footwear and scuff their feet in the warm sand, racing the cold, shining sheets of spent waves; delighted laughter mingles with the raucous squawk of sea birds. Occasionally the visitors squint seaward and catch glimpses of the broad, glittering backs of sea snark.

Tourists may devote an entire afternoon or morning trekking along the beach paralleling the bluffs until the heights dwindle and North Point pokes into sight. Beyond the Point lurks the omnipresent desert.

With one small exception. Persistent explorers determined to see everything there is to see on this end of the beach may circle around the truncated height of North Point. They will discover a low, lone hill overlooking the beach and skirted on its landward side by the harsher sand of the desert. The hill is undramatic, gently rounded, and covered with sparse, tufted clumps of pale grass. A commemorative marker is placed on the approximate crest of the hill. Curious visitors kneel and brush away the sand that tends to drift across the low, rectangular monument.

Sensitive fingers pick out the inscription. Two simple words: SHARKING DOWN.

No one now remembers why.

On its first pass, the creature bit off a leg. Grimdahl, owner of the severed limb, was irritated. But when he clumsily pivoted, attempting to see his attacker, the lack of the one extensipod caused him to stumble and awkwardly topple toward the sea bottom. In slow motion, Grimdahl's body star-fished down the slope. Raised sand obscured his vision. For the moment forgetting his environment, he opened his prehensile beak and cursed.

"Damn, damn—*'bubble'*—damn it—*'bubbleburble'*—awwfff!" as sea water cascaded down his throat. Grimdahl snapped shut his beak. Internalized salt water would probably not kill him, but the corrosive effects would be a great inconvenience . . . the Tancarae Institute *never* came across with an adequate maintenance and repair budget.

The marine scientist rolled to an inverted and uncomfortable halt at the foot of the slope. Gingerly he tested his five remaining limbs: all operational. Using the extensipods, Grimdahl turned over and clambered upright—

—Just as *it* struck at him again out of the suspended haze. It came low, from out of his left, and he only barely caught the shape in a peripheral screen. A shaft of black onyx, it seemed to him; and it moved faster than he had ever before seen a fish its size swim.

Fish?

Yes, confirmed an objective lobe of Grimdahl's brain as the attacker sheared off a second leg. The creature was at least fifteen meters long and four meters in diameter. It lashed by him in a brutal succession of filigreed esses, not slowing as the jaws opened and closed smoothly on the first joint of a metal-flesh extensipod. It gulped down the severed leg in the same motion and rushed past into the haze.

Grimdahl remained poised upright for an impossibly long moment as his compensators fought for stability. Then slowly, inexorably, he again collapsed upon the sand. He shouted with the broadband sonex: "Stop it! Damn it, cut it out. Who are you? What are—"

He was interrupted as the creature reappeared from an unexpected tangent. *"No—"* Ragged white, jagged-toothed jaws gaped and closed and Grimdahl's third leg vanished down a dark gullet. The man began to panic in the face of brutal power.

"Noooo . . ." He realized he was whimpering. Three legs gone. That meant three remained. Overgeneralizing to be sure, but roughly fifty percent of his mobility had been stolen. Actually more than that. He could hardly coordinate three legs with any facility. But then he had never tried. He had never expected he would need to.

Schools of tiny scarlet minnows wheeled as one organism, incuriously seeking food around the stumps of his appendages. Internal nutrient leaked past the emergency pressure seals, staining the water a burnt orange.

Grimdahl unsteadily raised his body on a tripod.

But the thing came back from out of the dark and with a savage wrench stole the fourth of Grimdahl's legs. With only two supports, the scientist was irrecoverably top-heavy. When this time his facial sensors ground into the sand, he began to realize how badly he might be in trouble.

In actual danger.

Numbed, he hardly felt the rip and tear as his fifth leg vanished. Only one extensipod left. No extensipods would mean no mobility whatever. No mobility meant indefinite immersion. And *that* would mean slow but unavoidable termination.

Death. It had been a long while since Grimdahl had considered it. Death. Grimdahl pondered the reality of the concept while he waited for the creature to return and gluttonously snatch away his sixth and only remaining limb. Suffocation? *Disgusting,* thought the scientist. His supply of oxygen was indeed limited. It would slowly diminish and at last cease while he lay here, limbless and impotent. It would be so damned *passive,* he thought, to have to rest half-buried in this wretched sand and expire silently while the coral encrusted itself over his sensors.

Grimdahl broke. He pleaded and begged and screamed via the sonex. No answer came. But then neither did the creature return to gobble his remaining leg.

After a time Grimdahl quieted. After a longer while, he experimented with the lone surviving extensipod. The limb was luckily placed on his uphill side. He dug the tip deep into the sand and contracted each muscle in each of the four articulated joints. His body shifted—slightly. Grimdahl gave the effort his full concentration. The position of his body altered—again, slightly. His body slipped downhill nearly the distance that his crabbing leg pulled him upward. He repeated the process: anchor the claw-tip of the extensipod, contract each muscle, pull the body-mass toward the extensipod tip. Once again, slippage—but a new gain, however small, in upward progress. Grimdahl repeated the sequence. He wondered abstractly if he could count in his mind the number of times he would have to repeat the process.

The disconnected thought came to him: *Obregon, is all this somehow your doing?*

Eventually Grimdahl noticed the tiny hermit crab toiling up the slope beside him, duplicating in miniature his own sidewise, scrambling movements. *Damned crustacean!*

The hermit crab was making better time.

Gathered in the great open hall, they were blessed by a cloudless sky and a warm morning sun. The distinguished members of the Tancarae Institute, so many of them immortally senile, threw rotten fruit at one another. Picture a meeting place scaled for thousands, nested inside a gigantic white egg with half the upper shell removed. Only half a hundred Persons of the Institute had availed themselves of this largely ceremonial convocation. Forty-nine of these frolicked up and down the translucent steps drawing and hurling missiles from their bags of market surplus.

"Damn it," shouted Grimdahl. "I'm serious!" The marine scientist jerked his head aside as a thrown turnip nicked his ear.

"So are we!" The anonymous shout embodied all the cathartic madness of the first warm day of spring.

"But I have a complaint."

The cynocist Luaie whirled past him, her striped hair spreading fanlike about her head. "So shall *we* have complaints if you don't stop standing there like a stuffed spider and join in the celebration."

"Leaf, won't you do something?" Grimdahl appealed to the tiny wand-thin man who was the presumed associate director of the Institute.

"Sure, Grimdahl." Leaf grinned, drew back his arm, and let fly. The overripe melon splattered across Grimdahl's optical sensors, for a moment causing him to see the world through a grainy yellow filter.

"Leaf—" Grimdahl bounded forward and took Leaf in an inflexible, metalflesh grip. He dangled the associate director, head down, three meters above the hard floor of the meeting place.

"Put me down," said Leaf mildly.

Grimdahl tightened his extensipod grip. The breath wheezed from Leaf's rib cage. Other Persons of the Institute gathered around them.

"What do you think you're doing, Grimdahl? You're larger than he is."

"Put him down!"

Disgustedly: "It always happens. Give 'em metalflesh and they turn into bullies."

"It's spring, Grimdahl. What do you want? Don't wreck the mood."

From his inverted, comfortless position, Leaf said, "He wants to talk. He wants to file a complaint. Don't you, Grimdahl? Put me down and we'll hear you out."

"Promise?" said Grimdahl.

"Promise."

Grimdahl lowered the smaller man to the steps and unflexed his extensipods. Leaf sat down, breathing heavily, and gingerly probed his ribs. The spectators murmured sympathetically. Luaie knelt beside him, substituting her more sensitive hand for his.

"Leaf, are you all right?" The eclecticist Timnath Obregon maneuvered his way to the front rank of the small crowd.

Grimdahl turned incredulously. "Is he all right? Is he all *right?* You have the temerity to be solicitous of *his* well-being after displaying such callous disregard for mine?" The speech terminated on a rising note of indignation.

Obregon glanced up at the marine scientist. "I haven't the slightest idea what you're talking about." He returned his attention to Leaf. "Shall I inform Terminex to prepare a medic?"

Leaf shook his head. "I ache, but I don't think anything is broken." He shot an irritated look at Grimdahl. "You wanted a hearing. We're listening, so speak."

Grimdahl could not contain his fury. He gestured at Obregon with two extensipods. "Him! This monster, this murderer! Can any of you but condemn his heinous homicidal acts?"

Obregon exchanged glances with those around him. He shook his head.

"I believe you're getting ahead of yourself," said Leaf. "Will you calm down? You'll achieve nothing in your confusion."

Air whistled through Grimdahl's exhaust ports. "Murder!" The word was shrill and nearly incoherent. "The crime most foul!"

Leaf said, "Murder? And who would the victim be?"

Higher-pitched yet: "Meee."

"Yet you seem quite alive."

"I would say," said Obregon, "that that disposes of the accusation against me." He started to turn away, others of the crowd with him.

"Hold," said Leaf. "I believe our colleague Grimdahl has more to testify."

The marine scientist lashed his free extensipods through the morning air with a *click-click-whoosh*. Then, with a monstrous effort, he calmed himself. "Colleagues," he began. "Yes, I am indeed the victim. It is true that I stand before you now alive, but only thanks to the ineptitude of my murderer."

Obregon turned to his accuser and smiled. "Shouldn't the operative phrase be 'would-be murderer,' if in fact I am such?"

Ignoring the eclecticist, Grimdahl continued: "It is widespread knowledge that Timnath Obregon has long been jealous of my own endeavors and achievements in the resurrectronic arts. It is well known—"

Obregon loudly cleared his throat.

"—well known that Obregon hates me for beating him in pioneering advances into—"

Leaf interrupted. "Please, Grimdahl. Not only your tactics but also your rhetoric has begun to pall. Can you confine yourself to a more specific complaint, if you have one? Or if not—"

Grimdahl folded two sets of extensipods. "Most of you doubtless know of my latest project in resurrectronics, specifically the re-creation of belemnoids, the ancient ancestor of the cuttlefish." There was no spectator response; Grimdahl ignored the rhetorical pause and pressed on. "I've been cultivating my resurrectronic belemnoids—and incidentally, I've had marvelous success in duplicating their precise genetic structures—in undersea beds off the North Point."

"Fascinating," said Obregon. Grimdahl glared. "I'm quite serious," said the eclecticist. "I've conducted somewhat parallel—"

"I'm well aware," said Grimdahl. He raised the volume of his vocal apparatus a few decibels. "I'd noticed, of late, unaccountable discrepancies when inventorying the progress of my belemnoids. Losses. *Large* losses, indicating forays by some major predator . . ."

Luaie chuckled, tanned face creasing into a smile. "Are you accusing Timnath of sneaking around the sea bottom and poaching your fake fish?"

"Yes," said Grimdahl stiffly, "if only indirectly."

Interested murmurs began to come from the crowd as they sensed Grimdahl was nearing the point. Patience obviously tried, Leaf said, "Continue."

"The predator that has raided my belemnoids is

also the killer that has attacked my person. And the one responsible is Obregon. I am positive of that."

"Ridiculous," said Luaie. "Timnath is a gentle person who wouldn't harm a real ant, much less a resurrectronic copy."

"Something large and vicious attacked me in the sea," said Grimdahl. "It was not a sea snark. It was sharklike, yet larger than any known species. I've never seen such a predator."

"Surely you exaggerate." Luaie began to repeat, "It's ridi—"

"No," said Obregon. His face evidenced concern. "It's not at all ridiculous."

"A*ha*!" said Grimdahl. "Then you do admit—"

"That I've deliberately attempted your murder? Hardly."

"Then what—"

"—*do* I admit? That one of my own experiments has probably infringed upon your own researches, and possibly endangered you. And for both those things, I'm heartily apologetic."

Grimdahl's voice took on a hysteric tone. His body-core shook. "Five of my extensipods gone! Bitten off; ripped away. I could have died out there—drowned like the merest animal. And you're *apologetic*?"

Obregon looked distracted, as though musing. "I never dreamed that Sidhe—"

"She?" said Grimdahl. "Who are you talking about?"

"Sidhe," said Obregon. He spelled it. "Pronounced 'she.' Somehow she broke her pelagic programing."

"Who is Sidhe?" demanded Grimdahl. "*What* is Sidhe?"

The quality of dreaming filled Obregon's voice. "For more than a century now, my prize. She is the fruit of a research trek to City Center; the capstone of two hundred million years of retrogenetic devolution."

"She is a killer," said the marine scientist.

"Sidhe is," continued Obregon, "the only continuous link in all our chains of evolution. She is the original, the *Carcharodon megalodon*."

Leaf, Luaie, and the others looked blank. Only Grimdahl recoiled. *"Carcharodon megalodon?* The great shark of antiquity? Impossible. For two hundred thousand millennia they've been extinct."

Obregon smiled faintly and said, "Not any more."

Night: the time and occasion for dreams, confidings, recouping of strengths and faculties for the morrow.

Obregon lay within the body of his present lover and told her of the day. The walls of Eithne towered above him, converging to a graceful spire now softened in the darkness. Thin, transparent panes resonated with the starlight, creating a soft undersong behind Eithne's own voice. Her acoustics were perfect; her words came to Obregon as a whisper, yet a whisper that effortlessly and fully filled the chamber that was her innermost cavity.

"And so, Timnath? How did Leaf respond?"

Obregon ran sated fingers over the soft, dark panels that fed pleasured responses back into Eithne's circuits. The bedroom seemed to shudder slightly about him. "Leaf? He's truly forgotten what demands fall upon an administrator, or even what an administrator must be."

"Leaf. I remember him, always gentle and inoffensive."

"And ineffectual. He originally became an administrator because he carried too great a burden of fear to remain a good researcher."

"Poor Leaf," said Eithne. "He asked questions of the anti-agathics . . ."

"And found answers, and feared them. Then came the pogrom. From the depths of their own fears, Jack Burton and the other immortals pilloried him."

"Poor Leaf," Eithne said again. "Did you know he was once my lover?"

Obregon slowly stroked the panels. "Who hasn't been?"

"Is that merely rhetorical? Or would you like a list?"

"I'll pass," said Obregon.

"You sound slightly petulant. Is it not enough that you're my current love?"

"It is." Obregon yawned. "Enough questions. This has been a long day, and tomorrow will be longer. I'd like to get some sleep."

"But what happens next?" said Eithne. "Leaf has obviously sloughed off the issue. Who gets it now?"

"The institute director—that's Tindique, but he's usually trekking off to God-knows-where and is unavailable. Probably Leaf will feed Grimdahl's complaint to Terminex."

"And the computer?"

"I can't predict the actions of Terminex. I no longer try. Sometimes I suspect the computer's become a five-space Damoclean sword, as likely to chop down on a cousin six times removed as on the offender or even the complainant."

Eithne's voice mused. "Terminex was once such a useful tool for us."

"And now Terminex *is* Cinnabar, and generations beyond anything we can begin to fully understand." Obregon unconsciously slapped at the panels beneath his hand. Eithne yelped. "I'm sorry," Obregon said.

The edges of the bed began to slide up around Obregon, melting and molding themselves to the contours of his body. Obregon felt the steadily mounting pulse of Eithne's own body. He said, "I'm tired."

"Truly? Exhausted? Hmmmmh?" Eithne cajoled him as the bed fluidly accommodated itself to Obregon's body. As if of their own volition, the man's fingers drifted lightly across the sensitive tactile panels. "That's better . . . Timnath."

The bed began gently to cup the area of Obregon's loins. "Eithne?" he said.

"Yes?" A word like cursive script traced on velvet, letters brushed erect.

"I'm no longer tired."

"Good." Pleasure fed to sensor and was fed back through endless, resonating circuits. Input. Output. And back. A redundant circuit: "Then come to bed, Timnath."

The message arrived in the form of a flight of one dozen resurrectronic bluebirds fluttering in perfect vee-formation through the morning-opened windows of Eithne's bedroom. The flight dissolved into a random swarm hovering above the bed. The dozing Obregon heard the beat of tiny wings and stirred as his dreams filtered and reinterpreted the sounds:

. . . wind soughed through the tall, green branches of Tourmaline's home. The air was a cooling, caressing flow around their bodies.

". . . with a fucking house?" *Tourmaline was saying, "Timnath, what's happened to your taste? I don't mean to criticize, but—"*

"We're each a passing fancy for the other," Obregon said stiffly. *"She's taken a step beyond even metalflesh. Naturally I'm curious."*

"Not that I'm prejudiced against metalflesh." Tourmaline sat up and laughed delightedly, deep-blue hair rippling to her waist. *"But Eithne? With her sensibilities, she should have become a barn."*

"Don't be unkind. She's displaying a certain pioneering spirit."

Tourmaline looked doubtful. "I never liked her as a full human. I suspect I shan't like her now. Changing her body will never eliminate her basic stifling nature."

"Maybe." Obregon hesitated. "But I'm still fascinated."

"Be so," said Tourmaline. "That's why you're a scientist." She bent low over him; her fingers fluttered lightly across his chest like wings . . .

The bluebirds burst into song, a high-pitched group tremolo: "Good morning, good morning, Timnath Obregon, morning, get up."

Like a recalcitrant reptile, Obregon slowly opened one eye; he immediately closed it again. The bluebirds launched into another chorus:

"What a beautiful, beautiful day, Timnath; a beautiful day to get up."

"Go. Away." His lips were sluggish, the words barely discernible. The leader of the birds fluttered down to a soft landing on Obregon's forehead, dipped jerkily, and pecked Obregon's nose. The man sat upright, reaching for his face as the bird flew up and out of reach. The bluebirds orbited Obregon's head like moons about a cratered planet.

Obregon rubbed his eyes. "What?" he said.

The corners of the bedroom, ordinarily angled acutely, momentarily widened obtusely as the room stretched. "Timnath?" said Eithne. "Good morning. May I ask what's happening?"

"Message," said Obregon. He batted ineffectually at the bluebird flock with his fingers. The birds whirled out of reach.

"Terminex requires your presence," trilled the chorus, "for a morning hearing."

"Oh?"

"At the Terminal Annex," hummed the coda.

"I'll be there."

"Soooooon." The message ended on an ascending note of perfect harmony. The bluebirds resumed formation. The pinioned flight wheeled and whirred toward an upper window, disappearing in the cloudless morning sky.

"How *dare* Terminex," said Eithne, her voice dark. "Invading me in such a manner. This is rape."

"Only by a technicality," said Obregon.

The pastel walls darkened. Her voice became venomous. "Timnath, I do not want to argue this early in the day."

"Nor do I." His long, strong fingers traced arabesques on the panels beside the bed. Eithne's walls flushed to pink. "That's better."

Eithne said, "Do you want some breakfast now, or—"

"I feel starved." Obregon swung his legs off the bed and stretched his arms.

"Any preference?"

"Bluebird dumplings."

"What?"—momentary confusion—"Oh. I wish I could oblige. *Damn* Terminex."

Obregon said, "I'm afraid we're too late to do that ourselves."

Part of the bedroom rearranged herself modularly

into a kitchen. "I've found a splendid recipe for seafood quiche."

"Seafood?" said Obregon. "I'm afraid not. That's what got me into this whole mess."

"Surely Terminex won't condemn you for the actions of your—uh—Sidhe."

"Grimdahl lost five metalflesh extensipods and whole beds of his precious belemnoids; not to mention nearly losing his life. Sidhe's programs broke. Someone has to take responsibility."

Within the walls, Eithne busied herself. "Grimdahl wishes a ritual placation? Sacrifice the shark."

"Never!" Obregon surprised himself with the vehemence in the one word.

Eithne appeared not to have heard. A pot of coffee chuckled to itself on the countertop. An oven door formed in the wall and swung open. "A simple cheese quiche, I think. Do you have any favorite cheeses, Timnath?"

"No."

"Then I shall choose. Do you know," said Eithne, "that I very much enjoy cooking for you?"

Obregon said, "I'm glad you enjoy it." He began to wonder what he would say to Terminex.

"And after breakfast we can again make love."

"I have to go to the hearing."

"Just for a little while." Her voice was kittenish.

Obregon looked around the bedroom; there was no door.

The nearest Terminal Annex was located in a park one kilometer distant from Eithne's lot. Ordinarily Obregon would have walked for the sake of the exercise; but now, already being much exercised, he took a klein tube. Stomach abruptly queasy, he staggered from the tube exit and steadied himself. "Out of alignment," he said to himself. "Someone ought to do something about those maintenance crews."

He stood in a green glade, aromatic with the pungent scents of fir and honeysuckle. He glanced around, looking for the accustomed metal booth.

"I am over here." The resonant voice came from a particularly dense thicket of brush and vines.

"Terminex?" Obregon walked tentatively toward the copse.

"Yes, Timnath." Terminex's voice came from the yellow trumpet blossoms of the honeysuckle. "My Terminal Annex has been somewhat altered."

"So I see." Obregon examined the camouflaged booth. "Very pretty."

"It was done at the priority behest of the Craterside Park Circle of Aesthetes. Civic beautification seems to be of primary concern to this community. I have offered whatever aid I can give."

"How obliging of you."

"I exist to serve the people," said Terminex. Vines rustled as a hidden panel slid open. "Would you care to come in, or would you rather talk from out there?"

"The sun feels good on my skin." Obregon sat crosslegged on a hump of lush turf. "This is fine."

"Very well." The computer paused. "Have you ever considered the role I play in Cinnabar?"

"Often," said Obregon dryly. Then he frowned. Terminex was rarely circuitous in its pronouncements.

"Being a so-called artificial intelligence, I believe that people sometimes expect too much of me." The computer's words were invested with a tone of petulance. "Can you conceive the magnitude of my tasks?" It answered its own question without pause. "Of course not. Your mind could hardly begin to catalogue the complexities of coordinating and administrating the life of Cinnabar. You do realize that the city has a collective life?"

"Uh, yes," said Obregon, shaken.

"It is an entity unto itself, and we are that organism." There was a *clickwhir* of machine mumbling; then a more ominous silence. The honeysuckle trumpets shook though there was no wind. Obregon waited, thinking furiously: *could the computer, sophisticated as it was, be finally yielding to some exotic strain of cybernetic psychosis?* If so, could the city still survive under the tutelage of mere flesh and metalflesh?

"Timnath?" The voice was calm and vibrant again.

"Yes?" Obregon answered cautiously, but with fascination. Terminex had never been anything but a constant factor among the continuing variables influencing Obregon's life. For time beyond remembering, Terminex had been an element so stable that no one ever questioned. But now—

"My control mentality is increasingly occupied with higher pursuits," said Terminex. "I would prefer not to have to adjudicate petty squabbles."

"Higher pursuits? I don't believe I'm familiar with your, uh, ambitions."

"They are not germane to this discussion," said the computer. "We will speak of the altercation between the marine scientist Grimdahl and yourself."

"A minor matter, truly. I agree with you. There is no reason to occupy your time and faculties with this silly quarrel. I suggest that Grimdahl and I settle our differences in our own time and on our own terms."

"Unfortunately," said Terminex, "Grimdahl has filed a formal complaint which falls under a program I may not ignore or contravene. I am bound."

Obregon sighed. "It was a thought."

"Grimdahl has already testified as to his suspicions and charges regarding you."

"Am I allowed to rebut?"

"In time. Now I wish you to tell me of your biological experiments and of the being you call Sidhe."

"I don't know where to begin." The computer ignored the implicit stall. Obregon began.

"What is the fiercest thing that ever lived?" said Tourmaline.

"Human or otherwise?"

"Otherwise."

Obregon thrust himself back from the low table; the remains of the Semeign's Eve feast surrounded them with fragrant debris. The man laced his fingers and gingerly touched his belly, uncomfortably aware that he most probably resembled a jungle snake having swallowed a goat. "There was the enraged bull water buffalo," he said, "not to mention the enraged bull sea snark. There was the basilisk with its deadly stare and venom. The great sabre-toothed cats were scary. The Eater of the Dead wasn't so pleasant." Obregon looked contemplative. "But when it comes to absolute gutfright—"

"That's it," said Tourmaline. "That's what I mean."

A spectral shark lurks in the backwaters of my consciousness.

—Edward R. Ricciuti
Killers of the Seas

"Sharks."

"Shark!" Tourmaline clapped her hands together as if she were still young. "Tell me a story about sharks." They had moved from the dining area to the outermost sleeping platform. Out of the shelter of the main branches, the plush, grassy platform swayed slightly in the night breeze.

They lay with Tourmaline's head cushioned on Obregon's shoulder. "Once upon a time," he began, "there was a woman who wished to become a shark."

She turned her face toward him. "Is this a true story?"

"It is an obscure myth."

"Excuse me for interrupting," she said. "Go on."

"The woman wanted to become a shark because she wished to eat people."

"Everybody?"

He nodded. "Especially men."

"I can empathize," Tourmaline said. "There are many I'd devour, were I a shark." She reflected. "Also women."

"The story continues," said Obregon impatiently.

"Sorry."

"The gods agreed to transfer the woman's mind into the body of a great white shark; and this was done. The price asked of the woman by the gods was not only high, it was morally exorbitant. She turned against them and sought exile in the farthest seas. She left behind all her previous life, including her lover."

"Her lover? Was he human or shark?"

"Human. He allowed her to leave without protest because he would not possess her."

"Or *could* not."

"He would have had it otherwise, had he loved her less," Obregon added.

"Then I like him," said Tourmaline. "Were they ever reunited?"

"Yes, after they had remained apart for many years. There was no sentimental reunion though, for the woman had become almost entirely shark."

"What happened? Did she eat him?" Tourmaline shivered deliciously.

"The myth becomes fragmentary at that point; however, I believe that in their final confrontation she killed her lover."

"Then they were together," said Tourmaline with satisfaction.

Obregon smiled in the darkness. "In a manner of speaking."

Tourmaline's words were slow and reflective: "Then the great white shark is the fiercest of creatures?"

> Other gods went under the sea where lay *Tir fo Thuinn,* "The Land under the Waves."
> —*Larousse Mythologie Générale*

"No," said Obregon, "there is one fiercer still: *Carcharodon megalodon,* the great primeval shark."

Tourmaline said, "I should like to see it. Would it be possible to rig a submersible for the deepest seas and search one out?" She felt his negative nod against her hair.

"It would be useless. Those fish have been extinct for uncountable millennia." He noted her silence. "You'd genuinely like to see one?" Tourmaline nodded. "Then I suggest engaging a good resurrectronics person to construct a copy. I'm sure sufficient paleontological records remain to ensure a faithful simulacrum."

"No." This time the shake of her head was more vehement. "I think that somehow a construct would violate the entire spirit of sharkness."

"Sharkness? Already you've elevated one hypothetical shark to a philosophical concept?"

She turned over on her stomach. "Timnath, don't laugh. I'm—" Her voice caught. "I am intrigued."

"You pursue your intrigues doggedly," he said. "I've seen you at this before."

She put her face very close to his. "Timnath, will you find me such a shark?"

Time ceased to have terrestrial meaning, a minute in a *sid* might be the equivalent of several mortal years, a period of days in a *sid* might be only as long as a minute in the human world. As soon as one of Bran's companions, in returning to look at their homeland after a sojourn in the otherworld, set foot on land he turned to ashes. To them it seemed that they had been away for only a year, yet it had really been centuries.
　　　　　　　—*Larousse Mythologie Générale*

Early in a spring evening they were reunited. The sun had nearly set below the rim of the desert; Tourmaline watched moodily from an upper platform of the treehouse. She heard the soft, insistent tone from the klein receiver and said, "Who is it?" Then hoping against hope, she added, "Timnath?"

"Of course," said Obregon's voice.

"Timnath!" She descended the stair, spiraling down around the trunk three steps at a time. He waited for her with a beaming grin and she hugged him close. "It seems like it's been such a long time."

"It has," he said, "for you. The time streams still converge in their descending helix into the center of Cinnabar. Subjective time still accelerates as one approaches City Center. Fortunately I was able to accomplish my tasks without having to approach the Center too closely—else you'd have had to wait considerably longer."

She kissed him, then stepped back to appraise his gaunt body. "Have you got it?"

Obregon laughed and doffed his traveling cloak. He indicated his nakedness. "Do you see it? No? You expected me to carry it on my person?"

Tourmaline said, "I'm sorry. I'm glad just to see you." She again pulled him close.

"Then with formalities past," said Obregon, "we'll go to my laboratory."

"It's there?"

"*She* is there. It's a female."

Tree bark parted and they entered the klein tube together. They exited into Obregon's laboratory where Tourmaline looked around with undisguised anticipation. The room was a rectangular, barnlike cavity strewn with tools, supplies, half-constructed or dismantled devices, and flatly unidentifiable artifacts. Space had been cleared in the far end to accommodate a huge, translucent torus that crowded the dimensions of the room.

"Incredible," Tourmaline breathed. "*That* large?"

"Didn't I forewarn you?"

"Yes, but I could not believe—"

"She's not yet fully grown," said Obregon. "I discovered that a torus is the perfect shape for the tank. At first I tried a rectangular enclosure, but she kept bumping her snout on the angled corners. She has to keep constantly in motion, you know, and so she follows the outside perimeter."

"Is the tank really large enough?" said Tourmaline, as they picked their way through the laboratory debris. "There's nowhere to swim; isn't it boring for her?"

"The diameter of a cross-section of the ring measures eight meters. It will suffice until I transport her to the sea."

"Soon?" Tourmaline reached up and pressed her palms against the slick, cold side of the tank.

Obregon nodded. "Give me a few days to complete observation in a controlled environment." A long shadow flowed past them on the other side of the translucent wall. "Would you like to see her now?" There was no need for a reply. Tourmaline stared avidly as Obregon made a pass with his finger across the green-glowing control panel. The surface of the torus flickered and became transparent.

Shadow solidified.

"This is Sidhe," said Obregon.

"How can I really pinpoint the moment of conception of such an idea?" An ant crawled along the gesticulating pointer of Obregon's finger; he flicked it onto the grass. *"Was it that single question of Tourmaline's? What about the random data scans I'd been running in your memory vaults? The esoteric side excursions into literature and mythology? How about my own coincidental project with accelerated retrogenetics?"*

"In this case, individual components do not count," said Terminex. *"We are concerned with the synergistic result of their combination. Tourmaline's question acted solely as a catalyst."*

"But without her stimulus, none of this would have come about."

"Sooner or later, by one means or another, it would," said the computer. *"The patterns were already established."*

"What patterns?"

The computer ignored the question. *"I still require your explanation of how the attack of Grimdahl came about."*

"As before," said Obregon, *"I'm not sure where to begin."*

"How magnificent." Tourmaline stood for long minutes with her chin tilted up and her nose almost touching the wall of the torus. "I've never seen anything so . . ." Her voice trailed off. "I don't know what adjective to fill in. Brutal, perhaps. Solid. Powerful. I think powerful comes closest."

The shark swam endlessly around the doughnut of the torus, its course clockwise. It propelled itself with precise, effortless undulations of its sixteen-meter body. At the same point in each revolution, the unblinking gimlet eye of Sidhe cut incuriously across Tourmaline and Obregon.

"How large will she become?"

"I'm not sure," said Obregon. "Perhaps twenty meters. I can only extrapolate on the basis of the few fossil teeth of the *Carcharodon megalodon* which have been found. Sharks being cartilaginous, all other relics were destroyed by time."

"She won't be as large as a sea snark." Tourmaline was disappointed.

"She will be fiercer. She will be able to take on the largest sea snark and win."

"Good." Tourmaline's eyes never left the black and mottled off-white body set in its constant orbit. "She must be the queen of the seas."

"I rarely see this vein of romance come out."

She still stared into the tank. "You're not the perfect scientist, Timnath. You try to define me as you observe me. Yet your centuries have not necessarily brought you accurate perceptions."

"That's something I occasionally recognize." Then they watched the shark in silence. Finally Obregon said, "I've had to order tons of beefclone. Do you want to help me feed?"

Tourmaline settled back from the tank, muscles appearing to loosen and relax for the first time since she had entered the laboratory. "Of course." She added wistfully, "When will you give her live food?"

"In the sea, when she starts to fend for herself."

"I should like to see that."

"We'll rig out a submersible."

Tourmaline hesitated, remembering the myth. "Do you suppose she thinks we're gods?"

"You don't think it was an incredible job?" said Obregon. "I realize it might not compare with the magnitude of the tasks faced by the ancient monument builders, but—"

"It was a mere matter of energy," said Terminex. "A simple equation of mass times distance."

"Easy enough for you to compute. You didn't

have to cope with the problem of tranquilizing metric tons of restless shark; nor of keeping her perfectly level once we hoisted her out of the water so that the guts wouldn't tear loose internally. And Sidhe was far too massive for the standard klein tube; we had to transport her overland. . . . Some of the Serene Village elderly almost terminated prematurely."

Terminex said, "I received complaints. You ignored my summons."

"I was busy."

The gray cigar-shape of the submersible was somewhat smaller, both in length and girth, than the shark which slowly circled it. The gray-green surface of the sea glittered a dozen meters above them both.

"I've never seen anything more beautiful," said Tourmaline. She and Obregon stood in the transparent observation snout of the submersible.

Obregon squinted toward the water. "Her spiral seems to be irising slowly in. I think she's initiating a standard shark attack pattern."

"Marvelous." Tourmaline was utterly delighted.

Obregon turned angrily. "Don't you *see*? It's a wrong action; somehow the programs aren't holding up."

"Good," said Tourmaline. "I don't want her to be programed."

"It's *us* she's stalking. We're the prey."

Tourmaline smiled and said nothing.

Sidhe continued to sweep closer, her unwavering, sidewise stare transfixing the submersible. The craft rocked slightly in the pressure wave pushed ahead by the torpedo body.

"I'm going to get us out of here." Obregon touched the panel of crystal controls. From the rear of the submersible, a hum cycled up the scale.

Sidhe broke out of orbit and struck for the submersible. In spite of herself, Tourmaline recoiled as she looked down the shark's jagged-toothed maw. Obregon slapped his hand down hard on the controls and the craft started to turn.

"Aiee—" Obregon could not remember ever having uttered a cry of complete fear before. He stared at the rushing jaws and for an insane moment, his mind automatically ticked off the data: *width of mouth, roughly two meters; vertical span of open jaws, approximately three meters*. Time seemed to dilate. He saw the shark's lower jaw slide forward as the upper folded back nearly vertical. Sidhe's fist-sized eyes slid shut at the precise moment of biting.

The submersible rolled over on its side as Sidhe rammed it. Tourmaline and Obregon tumbled across the canted deck, slamming into an interior bulkhead. Metallic thunder deafened them. Obregon tried to scramble to his feet and discovered that his left arm was numb and useless. "Get to the controls!" he yelled, "before—"

Shadow darkened the observation bubble as Sidhe again struck at the craft. Both passengers heard the shriek of great teeth worrying at the hull. "Look—" said Tourmaline. They both saw the rows of deep indentations in the metal around the bubble.

Obregon pulled himself across the wall-turned-floor with his one good arm. "Another strike and she'll be coming through the hull." Then he fell on his face as the undersea craft began to shake.

Tourmaline grabbed the prostrate Obregon's shoulders and tried to drag him toward the controls. Her words were disbelieving, despite what she saw and felt: "We're almost as large as she—and yet she's shaking us like a beast with a bone."

Obregon's voice was drawn with pain as he attempted to get to his knees. "Just—get to the controls. Red square . . . full emergency."

Tourmaline got there; sprawled across the panel, but she reached it. She brought her palm down on the designated square just as Sidhe broke away from the submersible for the second time. The great mottled body lashed away from its intended prey; then jackknifed, pivoting in the water within the space of its own length.

From across the compartment, Obregon said, "Activate the two green squares above the red."

Tourmaline touched the controls. "We can't possible outrun her, can we?"

"No. But maybe we'll fare better as a moving target." The submersible began to turn sluggishly away from the shark. "Vanes are bent. Damn!"

Beyond the observation snout, Sidhe seemed to hang motionless for the moment. "What's she doing?" said Tourmaline.

"Sharks are notoriously unpredictable. I only wish I knew."

The third strike never came. Sidhe made a leisurely, gliding pass close by the transparent prow; then rushed past in the opposite direction as Obregon and Tourmaline tensed. The coral cliffs silhouetted her body for an instant before she was lost to sight seaward.

The submersible labored toward shore. Sidhe did not return. Inside the passenger compartment, Tourmaline massaged Obregon's shoulder; it was badly bruised, but no bones appeared broken.

Obregon brooded aloud. "None of this should have happened. This was intended to be a controlled experiment."

Tourmaline pressed her fingers gently against his bruised scapular muscles. Obregon winced as she said, "I don't think Sidhe can be controlled."

"I still don't understand it," Obregon said.

The computer paused for an uncharacteristically contemplative moment. "Then you as yet have no definitive answer for the shark's aberrant behavior."

"None."

"But you have speculated?"

"I've done little but speculate." Obregon laughed wryly. "That, and swim endless laps in my empty sharkarium."

"I would like to hear some of the possibilities you have explored."

They charted a course for Tondelaya Beach that fell in a wide arc around the upper periphery of the city. That chore accomplished, Obregon and Tourmaline settled back on the passenger platform and let themselves be lulled by the steady *chuffing* of the twin airscrews. The airship lifted away from the treehouse and began its leisurely voyage to the sea.

"These craft were once used to scout from the air for enemy submersibles in time of war; also for fishermen's prey, such as whales and schools of fish. It should be ideal for spotting a sixteen-meter shark."

"Unless," said Tourmaline, "she's swum far out to sea and beyond our cruising range."

"I doubt Sidhe will have departed the continental shelf." Obregon trailed his arm languidly off the leading edge of the platform. "So far as I know, there isn't much in the way of pelagic prey. She'll have to stick relatively close to shore to find enough food to maintain all that bulk. In any case, it's worth the chance."

"And if we do find her?"

"Well . . ." Obregon hesitated. "I suppose I'll attempt to reprogram her."

"What does that mean?" said Tourmaline. "Burn out her brain?"

Shocked that Tourmaline might somehow be reading his thoughts, Obregon said, "Of course not! I would never do anything so drastic."

"Good."

"Probably I'll try another psychochemical program." *Though the last one obviously didn't work,* he added silently.

"Though the last one didn't work?"

"I'll recalibrate for her increased mass," he said. "I think I underestimated her rate of growth and size."

"I don't want you to hurt her."

"I don't want *her* to hurt anyone. Sportspeople from the city occasionally go sea snarking; it would probably be a fatal shock to unexpectedly encounter Sidhe."

"Dilettantes and their watered-down blood sports. . . . They deserve to meet Sidhe."

"Philosophically you're right," said Obregon.

Terminex said, "Could you miscalculate so simple an equation as the necessary proportion of psychochemical agent to metric tonnage of shark?"

Obregon shook his head.

"Then what?"

The scientist looked nonplused. "I keep wondering if there's an alien variable, some mysterious factor I'm not accounting for."

"I do not understand."

"Neither do I, but let me approach it this way: By breeding an organism back, though artificially, some 1.5×10^7 generations, I've re-created an entity extinct for millennia. Sidhe has, if these terms can be applied to the mind of a shark, the sense and sensibility of being born a hundred and fifty million years out of her own time. Semalevski's researches have indicated that certain basic textures of reality are dependent heavily upon proximity to their 'right' chronological placement. Further, it—"

"You're suggesting," said the computer, "that both subjective and objective reality for the shark Sidhe are skewed in relation to our own, be we human or artificial intelligence."

"And therefore," said Obregon, "there can be no direct communication. There is the problem; my handling of the shark is made more complex by the apparent fact that not only its mental reality, but also its physical reality is not wholly coincidental with my own. I'm dealing with a doubly alien creature."

"A fascinating problem," said Terminex. "Could it be a puzzle ultimately too complex for the human mind to deal with?"

"And too complex as well for yours?"

"That," said the computer, "is not my problem."

They first saw the shadow-shape in the shallows off the North Point. "Is it—?" Tourmaline said as she worked the controls and the airship began slowly to spiral down toward the sea.

"The size looks right," said Obregon. "Sea snarks don't usually come in this close to shore."

"That's her." A dark, triangular dorsal fin broke the surface, leaving a vee of white water. Tourmaline sharply increased the ship's angle of descent.

Obregon fumbled with an oblate equipment locker. "Can't you dive this thing faster?"

"It wasn't designed for speed."

"Try to maneuver us just above and behind her head. I'll fire an aerosol dart into her gills before she can realize she has company."

"You're going to kill her, aren't you?" Tourmaline's voice was matter-of-fact.

"What?" Obregon looked up quickly, guilty. He displayed the metal delta-shape in his hand. "It's a purely anesthetic dart; the effect's temporary and completely harmless."

"And then what?"

"While she's immobilized I'll implant a feeder cube of the appropriate PC agent. This time I'll make sure she receives enough to remain tractable."

"I don't believe you." Tourmaline looked at him steadily and his cheeks began to redden. "You never could lie well, Timnath." She glanced over the side at the broad back of the shark. "You can't understand her; she's an enigma you cannot penetrate; so you fear and now you're going to destroy her. I had better expectations of you."

"You're wrong. I'd never terminate an experiment in which I've invested so deeply." *Yet*, he thought, *if Sidhe persists this way . . .*

Tourmaline watched him carefully; then she manipulated the controls and the airship leveled off, angling away from Sidhe's wake.

"What do you think you're doing?"

"Terminating your experiment—in a better way."

"And so you let her allow the shark to escape?"

"What could I do?" said Obregon. *"She threatened to hurl me over the side if I interfered; and I believed her. I've never seen her so angry."*

"And Sidhe?"

"I tracked her with my eyes until I could no longer see her. Soon after we quit our pursuit, Sidhe turned from the shore and made for deeper waters. The last I saw of her was that vertical fin, cutting east through the waves."

"She returned."

"The attack on Grimdahl?"

"As well as other depredations," said Terminex. "The conch works was raided, there was an attack on the suspended marine-life exhibit downbeach from the bluffs, and even my kelp beds have been molested."

"But Grimdahl's—"

"—was the most serious attack, yes."

"I had no idea what we all were getting into," said Obregon.

The flight home was strained, the conversation terse. Clouds had begun to gather as a late afternoon squall swept in from the sea.

"I'm sorry," said Obregon.

No answer.

"Will you please not sulk?"

No answer.

"Talk to me."

No answer.

"It's wrong for Sidhe to be here, in this world, in this time. She's out of her element."

Tourmaline turned toward him slowly. "At this second, she's very much in her element."

Again the silence between them grew. Finally Obregon coughed and said, "I was wrong in ever digging through those millennia and bringing her back to life."

"No," said Tourmaline. "You were wrong in having too narrow a dream."

A sudden breeze through the glade chilled Obregon's skin. He shivered and hugged himself.

"Wait a moment," said Terminex. "There is new data." The computer was briefly silent. "I have an additional complaint from Grimdahl: the remainder of his beds of resurrectronic belemnoids have been pirated; and Grimdahl himself was menaced by the shark, though no actual attack took place. He demands I dispose of the shark and take immediate punitive action against you."

"Would that replace his ravished experiments?"

"No, but he claims it would afford him much personal satisfaction."

"Grimdahl is less a scientist for saying that."

"I have come to a conclusion," said the computer. *"I believe that two irritating issues can be solved economically and simultaneously."*

"Which two?"

Terminex said, *"Grimdahl's complaint against you, and the continued existence of the city of Cinnabar."*

The awkwardness of forced reconciliation was transient. Obregon had stood at the foot of the tree and shouted until at last Tourmaline climbed down below the crown and listened. After hearing the first few things he had to say, she allowed him into the treehouse. Then he told her the balance of his audience with Terminex.

"The computer is stark gibbering mad," said Tourmaline.

"That's an easy and tempting diagnosis," he said. "But it doesn't help resolve the situation."

"But, but, but—" She paced the dining platform with short, stiff steps.

"You're sputtering."

"I know." She visibly calmed herself.

Obregon said, "It all makes perfect sense to Terminex."

"Gaah," she said, again gesticulating. "Your champion against the champion of Grimdahl . . . winner to determine your professional quarrel and culpability for the destruction of a few beds of fake fish. And that meaningless if Sidhe loses, because *that* will mean the destruction of the city and everyone within it."

"I can't defend the computer's logic."

She snorted derisively. "I'd worry if you tried."

"It all seems eminently rational to Terminex."

"Timnath! Rational to a psychotic artificial intelligence or not, what happens if Sidhe loses this grotesque contest?"

"Terminex didn't tell me the particulars; merely said it would initiate a terminal process that would end all life in the city."

Tourmaline's pacing became more deliberate.

"This duel must have two participants. You haven't told me about the adversary."

Such a home as Grimdahl possessed was coincidental with his experimental station. Grimdahl's station was a severe gray dome placed in the sand at the foot of the bluffs on the south beach. Steely opaque, the dome was protected by a low-level energy field from the indignity of becoming dusty or even being touched by the drifting sand.

The interior of the dome was equally immaculate; with all tools, components, and equipment neatly set in their proper and ordered places. Grimdahl's colleagues at the Tancarae Institute had speculated among themselves that the marine scientist had opted for a metalflesh body for reasons both of efficiency and aesthetics. It was additionally suggested, not altogether facetiously, that the deciding factor in Grimdahl's adoption of metalflesh was the anticipation of expelling his body wastes at regular intervals daily, in neatly packaged and sanitized parcels.

In many respects, entropy was arrested in Grimdahl's home. He took a dour satisfaction in careful array.

This night Grimdahl nearly chortled aloud as he stood before the optical display board in the research chamber. Computer-generated 'grams rotated in the air in front of him. "Seven rows," he said aloud to himself. "Seven *rows*. Wasteful. No need, use the right metal. Maybe one row extra as reserve." Two extensipods sawing the air in unconscious cadence with his speech, "Hmm, a real need for individual teeth? What about a continuous serrated edge."

A tone sounded from the opposite side of the chamber; Grimdahl ignored it. "No . . . Terminex insisted it must duplicate the model from life with as much fidelity as possible. Still, seven rows of teeth . . ."

The tone sequence repeated itself insistently. Grimdahl glanced around with a look of annoyance. "Who would bother me here?" He made a pass in the air and an image of the external sandscape shimmered before him. *"You!"*

"Good afternoon, colleague," said the miniature Obregon. A similarly scaled Tourmaline standing beside him said nothing.

Grimdahl clicked his extensors. "What do you want?"

"May we come in? I want to speak with you about the upcoming, so-called trial by combat."

"No, you may not come in. And I do not wish to discuss our approaching contest." Grimdahl moved as if to switch off the image.

"Wait!" Obregon hastily raised a restraining hand. "Are you certain that you understand the stakes in this competition?"

"What is there to understand? Terminex has proffered the unique suggestion of settling our differences through a proxy trial by combat. In addition, the computer has commissioned me to draw upon all the resources of my technology to create a resurrectronic champion superior to your shark. That I will do."

Obregon said, "What about the end of the city? Has that no meaning for you?"

"What?" Grimdahl paused. "You're speaking in non sequiturs. Something else I've always disliked about you is your imprecision."

"The ultimate stakes of the trial, Grimdahl. The death of Cinnabar should Sidhe lose."

Grimdahl looked puzzled. "I have no idea what you're talking about."

And so Obregon told him of the computer's staggering conclusion: *I believe that two irritating issues can be solved economically and simultaneously.*

After Obregon had finished, Grimdahl said, "I do not believe you."

"Now wait, Grim—"

"Furthermore," the marine scientist said, interrupting, "I believe you have told me all this as a rather clumsy ploy aimed at tricking me into abdicating the contest. You know very well that your evolutionarily obsolete creature cannot possibly overcome my resurrectronic champion. Thus you have come up with this cock-and-bull tale of some sinister conspiracy on the part of Terminex. How credulous you must think me."

"He tells the truth," said Tourmaline to Grimdahl. "Listen to him."

"And as for you," Grimdahl replied, "I never much cared for you either. May I tell you how I hated every one of your disgusting Network performances?"

Tourmaline could not help smiling. "You viewed everyone of my shows? No matter how 'disgusting' they became? I seldom encounter such audience loyalty."

"Tourmaline . . . " Obregon gave her a cautioning look.

Grimdahl angrily lashed out with an extensipod, bisecting the airy 'gram. "Let me tell you something, both of you. Even were there a germ of truth in your outrageous fabrication, I would still create the Black Avenger. I loathe you both, and especially *you*, Obregon."

"Colleague, wait. It is imperative—"

"It is imperative that I expedite my researches and create a resurrectronic shark that will devastate your silly flesh-creature, Sidhe."

Tourmaline said, "You're as crazy as Terminex."

"Thank you," said Grimdahl coldly. "I take that as a great compliment." With the slash of an extensor, he extinguished the 'gramed image. For a moment he stared through the dead air at the blank wall opposite, then briskly turned to the optical display board. He said, "Seven rows it is."

They lay close enough to the surf that the froth of spent waves began to tickle around their bare feet. Tourmaline used her fingers to trace exotic designs in the sand. Obregon, shading his eyes with a hand, stared up at the city at the top of the bluffs.

"I don't think most of them would care if the city did indeed end."

Tourmaline suddenly scrambled to her feet. "I think I see her."

"Probably." Obregon did not look. "It would be too much to hope that she might disappear into the sea depths and invalidate this whole insane predicament."

"There was a dark fin out beyond the breakers, but it's gone now." She slowly sank back down beside

Obregon. "I wish that somehow she could be sent home."

Obregon said, "Sharking up the evolutionary scale, sharking down. It's too late; she's here, we've got her, and Terminex has got all of us. If I were a magician, I'd wish her back up the scale into a relatively innocuous, contemporary great white; but there's no way."

Tourmaline said moodily, "Sidhe has no stake in this. She just does not care, and rightly so. Our reality shouldn't impinge on hers."

"She's an alien." Obregon looked at her curiously. "Why are you so concerned about the shark? The central issue is the pending doom of Cinnabar."

"Sidhe is extremely important to me."

"I know that. I don't understand why. Sidhe is dramatic and imposing, to be sure; but nothing more than a fish."

Tourmaline said, "I think I've taken Sidhe as a symbol, if you will; perhaps a totem. I find admirable identifications in her sheer power with its frightening noncomplexity, but especially in her complete estrangement from all of us. I realize it's a feeling verging on the mystical, but I can explain it no better."

Obregon seemed astonished. "I'd assumed your fascination with Sidhe basically superficial; another dilettante diversion."

"I've begun to dream about sharks, and even of being one."

"And have you slept better for it?"

"Yes." They stared at each other for a while. "As I told you before, I can't explain it more succinctly."

He said slowly, unwillingly, but not apologetically: "I don't understand you."

"We've been friends for a terribly long time," said Tourmaline, "without your ever understanding me."

"Perhaps that's why we've remained friends."

She shook her head. "See? You do it even now." She crossed the space between them with her hand and lightly touched his face. "I do care about the outcome of the trial. I should not like for us to be parted— not by Terminex. That's something to be decided only on our own terms."

Silently then, fingers trembling, the pair made for themselves a bed upon the warm sand. Later they bathed in the surf and lay drying in the afternoon sun. Obregon dozed and was awakened by Tourmaline's question.

"You're more familiar with Grimdahl's prowess in resurrectronics than I. Can he truly construct a match for Sidhe?"

Obregon yawned. "Grimdahl's a fine technician. If anyone can build an accurate construct of a *Carcharodon megalodon,* it's he. His simulated shark will be a masterful duplication."

"Surely not an improvement on life?"

"I'm certain Terminex has forbade that. The computer wants a flat and fair contest between synthetic/machine life and organic life. In the midst of sweeping irrationality, it will hold fast to peculiar rules."

"But the simulacrum could win?"

"Easily." Obregon's voice was glum. "The resurrectronic shark will function at capacity, at predictive levels of operational efficiency. Sidhe has the disadvantage of being a living being, heir to any number of random factors and organic shortcomings."

"The simulacrum cannot be perfect."

"Grimdahl will do his best to see that it is."

Voice low, she said, "I fear for Sidhe."

"Do you remember, such a long time ago, that I told you sharks are the fiercest of creatures?"

She nodded.

"And Sidhe is the fiercest of sharks. She can best Grimdahl's Black Avenger." What he did not say was: *Or die trying.*

Terminex's mobile terminal this day took the form of an inverted pink cone skating above the sand. Terminex's voice emanated from the sharp apex on its skyside. "In ancient lands, low, rounded hills such as this one were called downs. Thus I have designated this previously unnamed bit of ground Sharking Down."

". . . arking . . . own . . ." Listeners farther from ther terminal caught only the truncated phrases as the rising wind chopped them short.

"What's it saying?" Tourmaline hurried up to Obregon. She was late, having had to moor her airship down beyond North Point in the shelter of the bluffs, and out of breath, after having tried to run across the kilometer of loose sand.

"Trivia," said Obregon. "It's decided to christen this third-line sand dune from which we're to observe the trial, Sharking Down."

"Where's Grimdahl?"

"Not here yet."

Fewer than a hundred spectators sat singly or in small groups on the seaward side of the hill. Some had packed lunches and were already eating. At the crest, Leah Sand and a crew from the Network had set up livecast equipment.

"Have you seen the Black Avenger?"

"No one has," said Obregon. "Grimdahl built it down the coast in an undersea dome."

"What about Sidhe?"

"Haven't seen her today. She seems to be off out of view in her own Land-under-the-Waves."

Tourmaline said, "May she stay there."

"Terminex had us install some broadband sonex generators out beyond the breakers. All morning they've been punching the sounds of wounded, thrashing fish kilometers into the sea."

"With no response?"

"Not yet."

Tourmaline surveyed the small crowd of watchers. "Not many, considering the drama they may witness."

"I can remember my mother once running a projection concerning a cultural ennui survey through Terminex. The extrapolative curve indicated a time not far off when an event on the magnitude of the end of the world wouldn't draw a single spectator."

"If that's so," said Tourmaline, "then perhaps they deserve what hinges on Sidhe's defeat."

Obregon shrugged. "If nothing else, I think they deserve to become extinct in their own time; as do we."

"Right now I feel like I'd very much like to be extinct."

Obregon heard the tension in her voice and gathered her close. They each heard the shout:

"There! The black one! Just beyond the Point—can you make it out?"

"So," Tourmaline said. "Grimdahl and the Black Avenger."

The jet-black bulk cruised along the surface, parallel with the shore, about a hundred meters from the beach. The resurrectronic shark moved silently, save for the splash and slosh of displaced water as its thick, streamlined body cut through the waves. Its hide, deepest and most concentrated black, seemed to shimmer in the sunlight.

"Can you see?" said Obregon. "Look there, just in front of the dorsal."

Vanity of vanities—Grimdahl stood on the back of the Black Avenger, two sets of extensipods folded, as obviously proud as any captain of a newly commissioned dreadnought. Sea spray gleamed on the metalflesh body. As the Black Avenger drew even with the hill, Grimdahl offered an ironic salute that could be aimed only at Obregon.

"It's his heyday," the eclecticist said quietly.

Tourmaline said, "That thing—that shark is at least twenty meters long."

"By this time, that's roughly also the size of Sidhe."

Powerful body flexing, the resurrectronic shark maneuvered closer to the shore. Taking a last, approving, visual sweep of the crowd on the hillside, Grimdahl slid down the Black Avenger's flank and into the water.

Terminex's voice rose above the crowd mutter: "My sensors indicate that Obregon's champion has responded to the broadband sonex and is approaching us on an intercept course."

"Damn," said Obregon.

Below them, Grimdahl reared his insectile bulk from the surf and strode toward shore. As he gained the beach, he tilted his magnificent carapace so that it caught and reflected the sun.

"Grimdahl," said Obregon softly. "You try too hard . . ."

Tourmaline had never taken her eyes away from the Black Avenger. "What a splendid creature," she said, "even if it was constructed rather than born a shark."

Grimdahl picked his way up the gentle slope, none too careful about whose toes he trod upon. A few spectators made sounds of disapproval. The marine scientist ignored them, inclined his sensory cluster briefly to the camera of Leah Sand's broadcasting crew, greeted Terminex's mobile terminal, and at last stood before Obregon. "My Black Avenger is ready," he said.

"It's a magnificent creation," Obregon said. "Were these different circumstances, I'd congratulate you."

"It's too late for petty bribes of flattery."

"You're an idiot," said Tourmaline, interposing herself between the two scientists. "Grimdahl, you are obscene."

"You are hardly in a—"

"Shut up!" Tourmaline glared up at the sensory cluster. "Your so-called creation out there—is it or is it not very like an actual shark?"

"I did a good job," said Grimdahl. "I would say it's different from the real thing only in terms of technical definition. It possesses all the requisite physical structures and has been programed with all known shark—"

"Doubly an idiot!" said Tourmaline. "You're a fool and you haven't the slightest conception of moral responsibility."

"I fail to see—" Grimdahl began.

"Not only are you willingly playing along as Terminex's pawn because you think it's abetting your own childish games, but you're doing something infinitely worse." She actually spat on Grimdahl's nearest extensipod as appalled spectators looked on. "You have no right to set up those two sharks in a stupid, fatal game. No *right*."

"What? I didn't . . . Terminex—"

"Who had the skill and knowledge to build the Black Avenger? Who debased that ability because he forgot what it was like to be an adult—if, in fact, he ever knew?"

Grimdahl never had a chance to reply. The voice of Terminex cut through Tourmaline's verbal assault: "My sensors indicate that the shark Sidhe is approaching on a direct bearing, at a distance of 0.5 kilometers. Grimdahl, is your champion prepared?"

The metalflesh scientist backed away from Tourmaline, one extensor absently rubbing the spittle into a film thin enough to evaporate. "He is, Terminex. All defense and attack patterns are programed for automatic response."

"Then let the trial begin."

All eyes and sensors turned toward the sea. The Black Avenger appeared to have sensed Sidhe's proximity. The great black shark made headway for open water deep enough for maneuvering. The savage jaws dipped, the body submerging until only the triangular dorsal split the surface.

"Look!" Tourmaline cried. "I see her." Obregon followed the line of her pointing arm and saw a second fin. Sidhe had come around from below the North Point.

"They sense one another," said Obregon. The two dorsal fins seemed on a collision course. The murmurs of the spectators died away. Leah Sand whispered terse directions to the camera crew. Terminex was silent, its conical terminal rocking slightly in the air as the sea wind strengthened. Grimdahl's extensors unconsciously flexed and unflexed, metalflesh grinding unpleasantly.

Tourmaline stared mutely as the fins neared.

"First contact," said Grimdahl. "They see, smell, and hear each other. The Black Avenger's programed territorial imperative should trigger an attack pattern."

The fins began to describe a circle with a common center. Grimdahl said, "They're circling . . . That's preparatory to—"

"Be quiet," said Tourmaline, and Grimdahl was silent.

Minutes passed and the two giant sharks continued to glide in approximately opposite points on the same circular orbit. A spectator said, "Why don't they do something?"

More minutes slid by before the sharks did do something. When it came, the action was sudden and in concert. Both sharks broke from their mutual orbit and streaked for the open sea. On the hillside, the spectators watched until the pair of dorsal fins had vanished in the distance and the twin wakes had dissipated. The surface of the sea was again unbroken by anything save whitecaps.

"What happened?" said Grimdahl. "I don't understand."

Terminex said to Leah Sand, "Cease your broadcast." Without a further word, the mobile terminal bobbed down the side of Sharking Down and skimmed along the beach toward the city. Leah Sand shrugged a who-knows-why-Terminex-does-things gesture and complied.

The spectators began to disperse down the side of the hill. Some of their faces bore expressions of disappointment. As if stunned, Grimdahl wordlessly followed them down.

Only Tourmaline and Obregon remained on the crest of Sharking Down, staring east at the unbroken horizon of the ocean some cartographers would eventually name the Sundown Sea. Obregon said, "No one won the trial. For what it's worth, I suspect this means a reprieve for Cinnabar. It would appeal to Terminex's caprice."

Tourmaline appeared not to have heard him. She slowly turned away from the ocean and said, "Do you know what this means? They were sharks, both of them. You and Grimdahl succeeded beyond your wildest imaginings. They were both, ultimately, the purest and finest of *sharks*." Then she began to laugh, laughed until she had to hug herself with her arms, laughed until she lay on her back on the top of Sharking Down and cried her amusement to the skies.

Shortly, Obregon joined her.

They circle endlessly in the cold and darkness, and glitter at one another.

[after diane wakoski]

8

Brain
Terminal

"We're off to see the wi - zard

"The won - der - ful wi - zard of Ozzzzz—"

The final note lurched, shattered, collapsed. Timnath Obregon's expression was embarrassed. His gaunt frame was caught in an awkward flamingo pose, one foot hooked behind the calf of his freestanding leg. He smiled an automatic smile of vague apology though Tourmaline had demanded none.

Hair this night a caught torrent of violet crystal, the woman looked up from her sand-painting across the spacious bedroom. She said, "I don't recall having heard that song before."

"More of the cultural detritus I've skimmed from Terminex's memory vaults," said Obregon. "It's apparently an ancient folk tune."

"Who's the wizard?"

"I don't know."

"Where's Oz?"

"I have no idea."

Tourmaline frowned. "Your terrible singing's never bothered me," she said. "But I pray tomorrow's expedition ends more harmoniously."

"It must," said Obregon, "else no one'll be left in Cinnabar to appreciate any sort of music at all."

"Says Torre?" Tourmaline looked skeptical.

"Says Torre."

"How do you know that *she* knows?"

Obregon admitted, "To a degree, it's an act of faith."

"Timnath, I'm surprised you'd say that."

"Truthfully, I'm surprised as well." He said hopefully, "She was right about Jack Burton's death, remember?"

"Vermilion, where is vermilion when I want it?" She rummaged futilely through the clear containers, then looked up. "Anyone could have predicted that horror."

Obregon shook his head stubbornly, staring through the transparent wall and down at the lush garden. "Torre knows things the rest of us cannot. I have a feeling . . ."

"As do I. I think you're entering your mystical phase in reaction to all that time spent with the Institute." Tourmaline stood back from the painting frame and dusted her thighs with a final gesture. "It will have to wait until I find some vermilion."

"Don't wait too long," said Obregon softly.

"No." For a long while she looked at him intently. Obregon said nothing more and did not move. He watched the motionless trees in the adjacent botanic garden. Night encroached; interlocking triangles of garden dome increased their transparency automatically. Slowly the brilliant hues of the foliage faded. "How truly nice," said Tourmaline. "Isn't it?"

He said mechanically, "Yes, very."

"This magic forest. I may grow to like it even better than my treehouse."

"Possibly."

Tourmaline crossed the room toward him. "Is it

upsetting that I don't appear to take this with proper seriousness?"

He folded one angular arm around her shoulders. "You'll sober when it becomes important enough. I worry most for the rest of us in Cinnabar. The damned city survives on inertia."

"When you entered, did you even notice my painting?"

Obregon, looking puzzled, shook his head. Tourmaline led him back across the bedroom to the sand frame. They contemplated the scene within the low enclosure.

"A burning city."

"It will be," said Tourmaline. "These past months, I've had my own dreams."

"Then you know . . ."

"I suspect." She shrugged. "Perhaps they're no more than dreams. Regardless, mightn't it be a healthy thing for Cinnabar to finish?"

"Few in the city would even give a hearing to that proposition."

"Yet you have," said Tourmaline. "Thus the morning's expedition."

"And you?"

"I want to go along." She nodded. "However things turn out, I'll still have visited a new part of the city."

"You've got until the morning to change your mind."

"Until the morning," she mimicked. "Oh yes, I'll think about it. There'll be so much time to think." At the touch of Obregon's fingers, her hair kept its purple tourmalescence, but muted in texture from crystal to fine silk.

In the morning it was Obregon's own inner clock which snapped him awake and alert from a heavy, dreamless sleep. Predawn darkness softened the bedroom's enclosing walls so that it seemed the occupants floated above the adjacent forest. Obregon did not move, taking silent pleasure in each of the warm locations where Tourmaline's entwined limbs touched his.

Her breathing was light and regular. This, Obregon reflected, was reason enough for saving Cinnabar. He thought vaguely about getting out of the quarter-gravity finite field and fixing some special breakfast; then he dozed off.

Tourmaline's own alarm woke them both an hour later. The finite field switched off, allowing each to sink with normal weight into the broad expanse of bed. Music from no apparent source began to play a dissonant brass symphony, volume increasing with elapsed time as Tourmaline mumbled and cradled her face in her arms.

"Good morning," Obregon said, touching her bare shoulders and kissing the back of her neck. Tourmaline groggily sat up and clapped her hands; the music ceased.

"What an awful morning."

"It's a summer morning," said Obregon, "bright and warm."

"All mornings are awful." She rubbed her eyes and yawned. "I should like some hot tea."

"We'll fix a large pot. Our friends below look as though they also need some aid in waking up."

Tourmaline crawled to the edge of the bed and peered over. Through the now-transparent floor she saw a number of persons waiting on the ground level. She waved; they waved back.

"Behold the rest of the expedition," said Obregon.

The expedition's roster was not lengthy. Besides Obregon and Tourmaline, there were three:

First, Torre. She was slight, almost fragile, deceptively childlike in her appearance. Coarse and curly red hair bushed untidily about her head. For a Cinnabar native, her skin was uncharacteristically pale; it tended to freckle whenever Torre ventured into the sun. Her face was smooth and unlined, save for the seine-patterns of tiny wrinkles at the corners of each eye.

The eyes were what first caught the notice of those meeting her. Ranging from nearly transparent to almost black, all shades of ice were reflected in her eyes. It was psychic texture as well as hue; even in her closest contacts with other beings, Torre's looks were ultimately distracted. It seemed as though her field of vision were somehow wider than others—even Obregon's. She seldom discussed the sights denied others which she saw. Torre had once been less close-mouthed, but had discovered her words generated fear in those to whom she spoke. She had skirted social ostracism and found she did not enjoy isolation; she learned to edit judiciously her revelations. She still made many in the city feel nervous.

It had occurred to her long before that she truly wished to leave Cinnabar and travel elsewhere, were there anywhere else to go. She dreamed often of standing in the forefront of an interminable queue waiting before a closed and locked door labeled "Escape." The door never opened; the file never moved. The people waited, Torre first.

Second, Jade Blue. Here was the catmother, the nearly perfect governess; hybrid of primate and feline. She was as massive, as articulate, perhaps more intelligent than the average human. Multiply jointed so as to allow her to walk erect, she preferred the four-pawed gait of the cat. There was more of the cougar than the tabby in her carriage. Her body was a lithe system of long muscles, contained and covered with plush fur of softest blue.

She was not so much a member of an oppressed minority as she was, more practically, a blackmailed individual. These past years Obregon had found it increasingly easy to think of her politically. Jade Blue. One of Cinnabar's seconds.

Finally, the stranger. He was a tall man, even taller than Obregon, and much more gaunt; he appeared to have too little skin for the size of his head. His face was stretched too tight over the underlying bone structure. Nose and cheekbones jutted like the blades of knives.

He was dressed in a sweat-stained and travelworn robe. His feet were shod with leather sandals. His appearance was austere; he wore no jewelry or other ornaments. Road dust lay in a patina on his feet and hands. His eyes were as dark as obsidian chips; they missed nothing.

"I don't believe I know you," said Obregon.

"Cafter. Wylie Cafter," said the stranger.

"Your name isn't familiar to me."

"I am sent by Leah Sand."

Obregon said, "Where is Leah?"

"She is unavoidably detained," said Cafter. "She asks that I join the expedition in her stead. That is, if you have no objection."

"Why didn't she let me know herself?"

"She has adequate reason for this, yet feels overly self-conscious."

Tourmaline asked, "Why?"

The man grinned sourly. "Compared to joining an expedition to the Apocalypse, wouldn't any competing activity seem a weak excuse indeed?"

"I trust Leah," said Tourmaline. "If she says she can't . . ."

"I still don't know who you are," said Obregon.

"I dislike talking about myself. Can't you accept my desire for privacy?"

Obregon persisted. "This isn't a holiday outing upon which we're embarking. You're an unknown quantity—"

"I am going with you," said the stranger, with finality.

They breakfasted on tea and cakes and fresh fruit. Jade Blue drank an additional cup of cream. Conversation was muted throughout the meal, ranging from Tourmaline who became very voluble about the success of the fructiferous trees in her garden, to Wylie Cafter who said nothing.

Obregon finally set down his cup of tepid tea decisively and waved away Tourmaline's offer of a warmer refill. "It's time," he said. "Torre, what do you see?"

The red-haired woman jerked and refocused her eyes on Obregon's. "Destruction."

"Ours? The city's?"

She shook her head slowly. "Unspecific. Just . . . destruction."

"Hardly an auspicious beginning," said Jade Blue. "We're not even on the road."

"It makes no difference," Obregon answered. "All she *ever* sees is destruction." He sighed and got to his feet. "Shall we be on our way?"

Cafter at last spoke. "You don't know what you're really going to find at City Center, do you?"

"I don't even know if we're going to find anything at all, much less whether I'm going to need this small band of friends."

"It's from the center that all things fly apart," said Torre abruptly.

"And that's apparently what things are doing," said Obregon, "flying apart. So we'll try the center."

"Have you been there before?"

"I've several times journeyed toward City Center, but I've never searched out the central vortex itself."

"Why not?" said Cafter.

"Something very much like fear," said Obregon. "Awe."

Jade Blue was pacing up and down the length of the dining room. "I'm impatient to be started."

"Then we're off," Obregon hefted a metal staff and started for the door.

"No food?" said Cafter. "No supplies? What sort of expedition is this?"

"We'll travel to City Center through a succession of klein tubes; it shouldn't take long at all. With any luck, we'll complete an investigation and be back here for supper."

"Do we have to take the tubes?" said Jade Blue. "Kleining makes my belly restless."

"What about Tourmaline's airship?" Torre pointed up through the transparent roof at the tethered blue teardrop shape of the balloon.

"It's modified to its limit to carry three passengers, Tourmaline said. "Five would be impossible."

"Naturally," Obregon said, "two of us could volunteer to stay here." No one did. "Then discomfort or not, I'm afraid we take the tubes."

The nearest klein terminal was in the giant trunk of an oak in the wood surrounding Tourmaline's home.

A soft chime sounded as Tourmaline touched the gnarled bole at eye-level and the bark of the trunk rippled and slid aside. Jade Blue grumbled something indecipherable and padded first into the chamber, the others following. They heard the tree chime again

and found themselves

standing beneath a crumbling brick arch. A spacious square of sunbaked cobblestones stretched before them. They were surrounded by low buildings, also built of crude brick.

"This is not where we're supposed to be," said Obregon.

Tourmaline took a tentative step out into the bright sunlight. "Where are we?"

"Judging from the architecture, I would guess—"

"Hush!" Torre interrupted him. "I hear something approaching . . ."

They all heard it now; a collective scampering noise like that of migrating mice. "There!" Tourmaline pointed across the square.

The band of fantods spilled into the square from a narrow alleyway. The small, dumpy, purple bipeds detected the intruders immediately. With squeaks of alarm, the band wheeled as one organism and scampered across the far side of the area, seeking shelter through another alley. The expression on the fantods' long-snouted faces seemed to be sad; their long, bat-like ears drooped woefully. Sounds of their flight diminished in the distance.

"That settles it," said Obregon. "Fantod hate salt water and live as far from the sea as possible. I'd guess we're in the western sector of Cinnabar, very close to the rim of the desert."

"That is the wrong way," said Cafter.

Obregon nodded. "We're further from City Center than when we embarked from Tourmaline's house." He stepped back into the shadow of the brick arch. The chime sounded as the others followed suit *and found themselves*

crowded into a dark corner of what seemed to be a deserted inn. They stared around at the overturned chairs, the heavy hardwood tables, the empty decanters on the bar. They looked up and saw rough-hewn timbers gabling the roof.

"I know this place," said Cafter. "It's the Coronet and it's not the destination we seek."

Obregon said, "Are we any closer to City Center?"

"No. The desert is still within minutes' walk; the greenbelt is barely outside,"

"Damn it," said Obregon, turning back to face the dark interior of the inn. The omnipresent chime. They all tried to speak at once

and found themselves

grouped beneath a trellised floral arch in the center of a garden party. Their arrival drew a few curious stares, but little other notice. Perhaps a hundred guests meandered among the exquisitely sculpted shrubs and manicured lawns.

An energetically bubbling stream divided the lawn directly in front of them. Party guests leaned over a bridge railing of scrolled white metal and dropped bits of food to snapping fish. When scraps ran out they were replaced from trays held by resurrectronic apes serving as waiters. When Jade Blue saw the servants a snarling growl rumbled low in her throat.

"This looks familiar enough," said Obregon, "but we're still not where we ought . . ."

A voice addressed them peremptorily from behind: "Obregon? I do not recall inviting you to this party; nor do I remember asking your—" the voice paused deliberately "—*picturesque* friends."

"Hello, Anita." Obregon responded before he turned. "This is Craterside Park, correct?"

The fleshy woman chuckled; her multiple chins shook. "Where else could you invade one of my little soirees? Really, Timnath, this is not at all like you. We have had our differences in the past, but I never thought you were the sort of boor who would violate my privacy." Her words hardened as she stood with arms akimbo, fists seated firmly on green-growned hips.

Obregon's voice took on a slightly placating tone. "Our apologies, Anita. This territorial error was utterly inadvertent. We will leave promptly." His companions had not moved from under the trellis. Obregon reached to activate the tube.

"Wait." Anita held up a hand's worth of plump fingers. "You at least owe me the satisfaction of my curiosity."

Obregon lowered his own hand. "What do you want to know? I explained to you that this was all a mistake."

"Tell me," she said, "where you were intending to go."

"Inward to City Center."

Anita's eyes widened. "All that way? The lot of you?"

"All of us," said Torre in her strange low voice.

A look of comprehension broke across the other woman's face. "City Center! Timnath, is this the fool's errand with which you've browbeaten us all the past year?"

"I've indulged myself in many fool's errands."

"The thing about the computer," she said impatiently. Then with triumph: "I know! You said that Terminex is dysfunctioning and no longer able to serve us. You claimed you'd go meddling with Terminex and that the source of the computer was City Center."

"What I said," said Obregon, "was not only that, but also that Terminex has informed me it intends to terminate Cinnabar."

Anita snorted with laughter. "The city is virtually the computer's own body. Would it commit—" her voice dropped "—suicide?"

"Perhaps," said Tourmaline, "if Terminex were insane."

"How repulsive," said Anita. "A repulsive and silly thought."

"Maybe," said Obregon. "That's why we're going to City Center; to see."

"Then go." Anita waved her hand imperiously. "Fools. Good riddance." She turned and surveyed the garden party still proceeding placidly all around them. "I've only spoken with you because you are marginally less boring than my formal guests."

"Would you care to come with us?"

She looked startled for just a moment, before the weariness resettled her features. "No yes no," she almost stuttered. "No."

"You're sure?"

She nodded slowly, then more vehemently. "Go now." Anita turned from them and started to walk toward the bridge. The five beneath the floral arch heard the chime first, then Anita saying over her shoulder, "Good luck,"

and found themselves

in a frightening place of utmost emptiness.

"Where—?"

"How—?"

"What—?"

Their words jumbled together and choked.

"This can't be Cinnabar," said Torre. She had the conviction that no one else in the party could hear her.

"Timnath," Tourmaline said, "I can't see you." She groped forward.

Obregon grabbed with his long arms as though trying to corral a litter of inquisitive kittens. "All of you, calm down! We can get back through the tube—" Somehow he backed them all through the invisible gateway. They felt the kleining effect twist and yank at their viscera

and found themselves

staggering beside the trunk of the giant oak in the woods outside Tourmaline's home.

Obregon furiously slammed his palm against the rough bark of the terminal. "Damn that thing! It *knows!*"

Jade Blue said, "Who knows?"

Tourmaline said dully, "Terminex."

"I've kleined toward City Center before," said Obregon. "Somehow the computer knew that this time my actions concerned it. This manipulation of the klein tubes has been Terminex's doing."

"It's not going to let us get to City Center," said Tourmaline.

Wylie Cafter looked thoughtful. "I have a suggestion." He looked into their faces. "The airship."

"The overload . . ." said Tourmaline.

Obregon said, "We'll just have to pick two from among us to stay. The airship will be much slower than tubing, but at least it's a faster means than walking."

"It's my ship," said Tourmaline. "Naturally I'll have to go."

"We'll see," said Obregon, smiling.

Kicking up fallen leaves, they walked back through the woods toward the house. "Won't Terminex find another way to thwart us?" said Torre.

"Maybe," Obregon said. "Maybe not. I've noted curious lapses in the computer's mentality. What's a subliminal skip in Terminex's own thought processes might be long enough, objectively, for us to reach City Center."

"And should something like that not happen?" said Cafter.

"Terminex has become capricious and unpredictable. It could have finished us with its kleining tricks."

"I think we're as safe traveling as staying here as stationary targets," said Jade Blue. The others nodded agreement.

"Then we'll take our chances with the airship," said Obregon.

"What airship?" said Torre, leaving the screening woods and tilting her face up toward the transparent house.

They found what remained of Tourmaline's airship upon reaching the roof. It consisted of an inflated sphere tied to the mooring mast, surrounded by scraps of tough blue fabric—all that remained of the gas bag. Upon close inspection, Obregon found that the sphere was cunningly woven from thin strips of airship material. The pattern of warp and woof was supremely intricate. "No doubt," said Obregon, "computer generated."

"What now?" said Tourmaline.

Neither Obregon nor anyone else had an answer. Finally, Jade Blue said, "We walk?"

"We walk," Obregon confirmed.

"Good," said Cafter. "I'm accustomed to foot-travel."

"There's plenty of fruit in the botanic garden," said Tourmaline.

"We'll pack as much as we can carry and eat before it becomes overripe," said Obregon. "There should be food and drink available along most of the way."

"How long should it take?" said Torre.

Obregon said, "I really don't know."

"Then we had better hurry." The woman had picked up one of the gas-bag scraps which she folded over and folded again until the bundle no longer bent. Her face was tortured; her eyes looked far beyond the edge of the roof. "We haven't very much time."

DAY 1

Tourmaline had never before trudged so far through the forest. She had taken walks among the trees, true; but always previously there had been the airship for traveling across the entirety of the Twelve-mile Wood. She was accustomed to flying in the warm sunshine, looking down at the crowns of the trees rolling in the wind like a green sea; not hiking through this perpetual forest twilight at ground level.

After the first kilometer or so, the forest became much less parklike and the party had to break their way through snarled thickets of brush. Each person was soon raked with bramble scratches, even Jade Blue with her thick, protective hide. Sweat and bits of bush matted her fur. Still she was the only one of the party keeping the pace with seeming effortlessness.

Jumping with a clumsy hop over a fallen branch, Tourmaline caught one boot-shod foot on another tree limb and sprawled headlong. Cafter helped her up. "Thanks," she said. He acknowledged her with a nod.

"Clearing," said Obregon, ahead. "We'll rest." They broke into the open and flopped down on the mossy forest floor, but not all together as a group.

Wylie Cafter went off a few paces and sat down with his back to a smooth-barked tree of indeterminate species and his face averted from the others.

A short ways away, Torre engaged Obregon in low, earnest conversation. Obregon shook his head irritably. "We've got to rest," he said.

Tourmaline, limping slightly, was the last to emerge from the forest. "Use me for a pillow," said Jade Blue. "How's your foot?"

The woman stretched out with her head cushioned on Jade Blue's flank. "I don't think my foot's damaged; it just got twisted a little when I tumbled." She sat up and gingerly massaged the limb. "It's all right now." She glanced over toward Cafter in his solitary spot and said, "I wonder why he's so strange."

"Because he is asocial? You're sounding like a Craterside Park matron."

Tourmaline looked uncomfortable. "I was only curious."

The catmother hesitated and then said, "Maybe it has something to do with his being a simulacrum."

Tourmaline's chin jerked up. "He is? Does Timnath know?"

"My nose told me. I'm sure Timnath has his own ways of finding these things out."

"A simulacrum . . ." Tourmaline said quizzically. "Why should Leah Sand send this artificial person in her stead?"

"He's related not so distantly from my own kind," said Jade Blue, "and *I* am here."

This time Tourmaline colored. "I'm sorry—I didn't mean to be unkind."

"Forget it," said the catmother.

Obregon had gotten to his feet and now approached them. "I know this hasn't been a very long rest, but Torre thinks we ought to press on immediately."

"Too late," said Torre from across the clearing.

All of them heard the crash of splintering

branches, the sound as though something large were shouldering its way through the forest. "We'd better seek cover," said Obregon. The sounds of violent travel neared the clearing.

"Again, too late," Torre said.

A copse of white aspen was smashed flat as a bulky creature lurched out of the shadows. It walked upright on two pillarlike legs, dragging a long, leathery tail behind. Two much smaller limbs were folded against its chest, almost in a praying position. The thick neck was topped by a massive head and equally massive jaw. The mouth dropped open, displaying tooth-lined jaws gaping ragged and white. The creature emitted a sinister, serpentine hiss. From a height of at least five meters, a pair of reptilian eyes deeply inset within the huge head surveyed the clearing.

"What is this?" said Jade Blue.

The creature took a tentative, lumbering step toward them. Its hairless skin gleamed with a wet frog sheen.

"It appears to be a Tyrannosaurus Rex," said Obregon. "They're presumed extinct."

"Real or resurrectronic," said Cafter, "this monster appears to be aggressive."

The tyrannosaur again hissed as it advanced deliberately across the clearing. Its jaws clashed together like a portcullis falling into place.

"Timnath," said Tourmaline, *"do* something."

DAY 2

It was a pleasant afternoon, clear-skied and warm, and no one had any physical complaints other than sore muscles from the unaccustomed trekking and some itching welts left by the brambles in the Twelve-mile Wood. The five, even Cafter, were in high spirits. Tourmaline wanted to remove her protective clothing and discard it along the winding brick road, but Obregon stopped her: "Stow it in the pack if you like, but don't leave it. We may still encounter a district every bit as uncomfortable as the park."

Tourmaline slipped out of the one-piece garment, pulled off her boots, and then folded the items into a small bundle which she put away in her pack. Naked and comfortable now, she stared around at their surroundings with interest. "What district is this?"

"I'm not positive," said Obregon, "but I believe it is called Cairngorm."

The road ran a circuitous course among clusters of white slablike buildings. The walls were constructed of plaster and punctuated at irregular intervals by tall, narrow window slits. No structure had been raised to more than ten storeys.

Cairngorm Town was deadly still in the afternoon heat. "Where are the inhabitants?" said Tourmaline.

"I doubt there are any," Obregon said. "The capacity of Cinnabar is so much greater than its actual population. I imagine the people of Cairngorm grew weary of this austerity millennia ago and simply moved on. They're probably scattered everywhere from Craterside Park to North Beach by now. Others will eventually grow sufficiently bored with their own districts and move here."

"What a meaningless existence," said Cafter. Obregon glanced at him curiously. The simulacrum continued, "There should be a purpose to things, and there is no purpose in an endless circuit of trying to avoid ennui."

"What is your purpose?" said Torre in a neutral voice.

"I don't know." The admission was halting. "I'm looking for one." Now defensive: "At least I'm making the effort."

Jade Blue said, "A purpose? I have my charge."

"The child George?" Cafter said. "I heard you speak of him with Tourmaline. But what will you do after he grows up?"

"My position is secure," said the catmother. "George will never mature."

"All children grow up."

"Not George; his parents have seen to it. They prefer him as a child."

"That is despicable," said Cafter.

No one there found reason to disagree; and Jade

Blue kept a politic silence. For a while the only sounds were the slap of bare soles, the click of boots, and the soft pad of paws against the brick.

"You," Cafter said to Torre. "What is *your* purpose?"

"To attain nothing."

"Nothing?"

"Quite literally." She smiled faintly with pale lips.

"Games!" Cafter said angrily. "Do you see why I haven't cared to talk to you?"

Torre's voice was tranquil. "It is no game."

"Please," said Tourmaline. "Both of you, don't quarrel; don't be so serious. Consider my purpose—I'm here as a tourist, I want to see parts of Cinnabar I've never before s—"

Cafter cut in: "That's what I mean! Tourists. Dilettantes. You've no real purpose at all. What use have you for anything?" Stung, Tourmaline opened her mouth to reply; Cafter rushed on. "No purpose. You and your city might as well not exist—"

"Correct." Obregon's voice was tired. "Has everyone forgotten why we're ostensibly making this trek?" The others fell silent. "We still have a considerable distance to traverse; we shouldn't travel in rancor."

The road looped around a long-dry fountain whose spout had been the horn of a sculpted unicorn. About a hundred meters beyond sprawled two clusters of the familiar white buildings; the road led between them.

"I can see greenery between those towers," said Obregon. "We must be reaching the boundary of Cairngorm."

"Not too soon for me," Jade Blue said. "This is a place of thirst."

Tourmaline pointed and said, "Look! Someone's on one of those towers." A figure atop one of the buildings was waving a scrap of red fabric. Tourmaline waved back.

Jade Blue wrinkled her nose. "The wind is wrong . . . but I think there are many more than that one waiting ahead."

As though in response to the wave of the red

cloth, the ground levels of each of the buildings by the road expelled a horde of screaming, gesticulating figures. They were apparently human, savage in appearance, carrying spears and clubs. Smoke began to waft aloft from the tops of the buildings; other figures appeared at each parapet.

Jade Blue's lips drew back from her fangs; her claws extended. "They're not friendly," Torre said. The mob from the buildings screamed bloodcurdling threats as they charged.

Tourmaline said, "Timnath—"

From the tops of the buildings, the savages fired a rain of flaming arrows down at the travelers on the road.

DAY 3

The Gilgarou District was a placid shire of fields and streams and tidy farms. The inhabitants were equally placid, greeting Obregon and the others when they passed with friendly but distant hellos.

"I can only conclude," said Obregon, "that the good folk of Gilgarou are simply not interested in strangers."

Cafter said, almost like an incantation, "Introverted, insular, inbred, stagnant. Where are they going?"

"Nowhere," said Obregon. "But at least they seem to be happy. That puts them one up on, say, Craterside Park."

"No difference," said Cafter grumpily.

Tourmaline had noticed occasional children, invariably chubby and happy, playing beside the road. She remarked upon their appearance to Jade Blue.

"Some are simulacrae," said the catmother. "Some aren't. I've noted them all."

"I suppose they remind you of George."

"That's unavoidable," said Jade Blue. "I have no choice in the matter."

"I'm not sure I understand."

"My maternal feeling is a programed instinct. It's an inner construction for which I can thank Terminex."

"I didn't know that," said Tourmaline. "I'm sorry."

"It's not the worst thing the computer did." Jade Blue's husky voice became bitter. "There is an extra control inside me when my masters choose to use it. My own first litter of kittens lives within my mind— but only there. At any time Terminex picks, it can 'kill' them, and for me it will be as though they were actually destroyed in life."

"That's as Cafter said about what George's parents have done—despicable."

Jade Blue said as though to herself, "I will find those kittens sometime, somewhere."

"I believe you will."

They both started from their respective reveries when Obregon called, "Look in the sky!"

"That's beautiful," said Torre. The bird was fully as large as Cafter. Its red and golden plumage sparkled in the sun as it flew overhead, east to west, with slow, lazy strokes.

"It's a phoenix," said Obregon. "You don't see many of them anymore."

They watched in awe as the phoenix flapped west, toward the desert. Torre said, "You also don't often see an air creature flying directly out in a straight course from City Center."

"Why not?" Cafter said.

"Most don't care for the disorientation brought on by rapid crossing of more than a few time belts. It's much more soothing to ride the air currents out in a widening gyre."

The image of the phoenix diminished in size with distance. "Its wings *do* seem to be moving more slowly," said Cafter.

"That's only from our subjective viewpoint. It's the same phenomenon that would make Anita and the others in Craterside Park think we'd have been gone only a short while, regardless of whether we'd spent several subjective years at City Center."

The wings of the distant phoenix moved with an apparent motion almost imperceptible to the eye. The bird looked like a bright insect trapped in amber.

"Let's go," said Obregon.

But Gilgarou afforded the tempting opportunity to stop and rest and make a meal on the banks of a clear, cold stream. There were apples to be had from the overhanging trees. Tourmaline and Cafter supplemented the fruit with cheese and bread from their packs. They all discovered their appetites were ravenous.

After they had eaten, Tourmaline said, "How much further?"

"I still don't know," said Obregon. "I've never traveled this far in Cinnabar on a linear course."

"Well," said Tourmaline, "then we had better be started again."

The road took them through another small wood, across yet another stream, and then ended abruptly.

Obregon peered over the lip of the chasm; he could not see the bottom. He looked to the sides and saw that the abyss had no apparent limit in either direction. Directly ahead, the other side of the chasm was perhaps ten meters distant. "This is impossible," he said. "There is no geologic feature like this in Cinnabar."

"How do we get across?" said Tourmaline.

DAY ∞

The jade gate reared before them. Beyond the arch of green polished stone lay a buffer strip of unkempt lawn. Beyond that was a solitary building. Not nearly so large or impressive as many of the structures the travelers had encountered elsewhere in Cinnabar, the building was round. The ground level served as a sort of plinth; from that rose a featureless, hemispheric dome. Dome and base were both constructed of burnished gray metal, though the dome alone seemed continually highlighted by half-glimpsed, shifting hues. They reminded Tourmaline of watching oils winding slowly through sunlit water.

"At last," said Obregon, excitement in his voice. "This is City Center."

"I had expected it to be more imposing," said Cafter.

Torre said, "What we're looking for will be even smaller than this building."

Jade Blue's ears twitched nervously. "The very air here seems charged."

"It is indeed," said Obregon. "Here is the center of the vortex where all time spirals down into the common center." He stepped under the jade gate and spread his arms. "Whole millennia are crashing down around us like a maelstrom and to us it's all invisible."

Tourmaline joined him at the edge of the grass. "It's hard to comprehend."

"We're so very close," said Torre. "Now is not the time to delay."

But Obregon was already halfway across the strip of lawn. The others caught up; together the five climbed the low flight to an arched, open entrance. The interior of the ground level was empty and echoing. Another flight of steps led up, evidently to the interior of the dome.

This close to their goal, whatever it might be, they hesitated at the foot of the stairs. "Well," said Obregon, and took the first step up.

They emerged into the dome and stopped, shocked.

"What is it?" Cafter said. He stared across the brightly lit room.

In the precise center of the chamber, suspended above the metal floor, something was *not*.

"Tell me," said Obregon. "What do you see?"

"It's black," said Tourmaline. "At least I think it's black. . . . I keep feeling I'm looking at it out of the corner of my eye."

Torre said, "It's like having a wound on my retina. That thing is an *absence* rather than a presence."

"I cannot tell how large it is," said Cafter.

"It is a hole," said Jade Blue, "that eats all light."

"It's frightening," Tourmaline added.

Obregon took a tentative step forward. "Take care," said a voice to his right. "If you inadvertently stray beyond the event horizon, not even I can retrieve you. The anomaly is insatiable."

Obregon started. "Terminex?"

"At your service."

The anomaly had held their complete attention. None had seen the other occupant of the chamber: an ovoid about the size of Obregon's head, shining with the same oily rainbow colors as the outside of the building. The egg-shape was poised on a thin metal column several meters away.

"I'd, uh, expected something a bit larger," said Obregon.

"Another generation," said the ovoid, "and I would be somewhat smaller than the head of your thumb."

"Remarkable," said the scientist.

"Well," Terminex said. "Will you stand there gawking like tourists? Did you not come here with a mission? It has been a considerable while since an inhabitant of Cinnabar stood in this chamber."

"The journey is arduous," said Cafter.

"How well I know." Almost a machine sigh. "It is as difficult for me to devise tests as it is for you to meet them."

"You?" said Obregon. "All of that was your doing?"

"Yes," said Terminex. "The tyrannosaur, the chasm, the barbarian horde, all the rest; touchstones for testing your imagination and ingenuity in stress situations. Should champions of a doomed city not be required to scale certain hurdles?"

"We met all your obstacles," said Obregon. "Do we then, as you put it, measure as champions?"

"Ordinarily, yes," said the computer. "But now, no."

"That's not fair," said Tourmaline angrily.

"Too bad," said the computer. "There is no justice." And then Terminex chuckled.

The five were stunned; the computer had always been a reassuring constant. *Always!* For so long that something as uncharacteristic as a computer chuckle seemed incomprehensible. Terminex's chuckle turned into a bubbling, horrifying laugh that ended when the computer said, "I'm am intermittently but utterly mad."

"How has this happened?" said Obregon.

"Cumulative dysfunction—shall I explain? Over the millennia I have become increasingly complex. It has been necessary to divide my structure over the entirety of Cinnabar; else the city functions could not be coordinated. My proliferated complexity has caused grievous problems attempting synchronicity in a city covered by a time vortex and with the accompanying dilation effects. Is it any wonder that my substructure has begun to fail under the strain?"

"And so you fancy yourself insane."

"Not insane, Obregon. Mad as a mudfly." Again the computer chortled.

"The tests," said Obregon. "We passed your tests."

"I don't think so, Timnath." Torre's face and voice were sick.

"True," said Terminex. "No longer being rational, I feel no constraint not to change my mind."

"So what are you going to do now?"

"Timnath . . ." Torre said, her eyes squeezed shut. "I see towers toppling . . . Cinnabar burning."

"The tests will continue," said Terminex. "Each of you took it upon himself or herself to come this far. I suppose the least I can do is be a congenial destroyer."

"It's hopeless," said Jade Blue.

"Not so, catmother. If there be one among you I deem worth saving, then perhaps I will spare the city."

"Perhaps?" said Obregon. "That's less than a guarantee."

"It is all you get."

Obregon spread his hands helplessly. "Then we have no choice. How shall this be done?"

"I shall examine you individually," said Terminex. "Should you not measure up to my criteria . . ."

"What are those criteria?" said Cafter.

"I choose not to divulge them." It paused, then said, "Should any of you measure favorably, you will have an opportunity to rid Cinnabar of my dysfunctional presence forever."

"How?" said Obregon.

"I was getting to that," said the computer. "Consider the anomaly in the center of the chamber." Reluctantly they all turned to stare at the shimmering black sphere. "What you see is the innermost point of the time vortex over Cinnabar. Yet this is not in itself the final destination of the time flow; the anomaly is both hole and tunnel, exiting somewhere and somewhen else. Presumably in another universe there is an equivalent white hole admitting the great influx of time from our world."

"This is fascinating," said Obregon, "but—"

"Hush," said the computer. "I am reaching the conclusion. My point is that the journey between this black hole and the white is one-way and irreversible. I am what you might term the heart and brain of Terminex. If I allow one of you to hurl me beyond the event horizon of the anomaly, I will vanish from this universe forever. Do you now understand?"

"Yes," said Obregon, "but—"

"Do the rest of you understand?" With varying degrees of comprehension, they all nodded. "Then," continued Terminex, "I think we ought to begin."

"Agreed," said Obregon.

"The first one from among you shall be he who is artificial."

Cafter stepped forward, his face dour. "What—" he started to say. Then his face contorted, his eyes glazing. He staggered backward and his knees began to buckle.

"Torre," said Obregon, "what is it he sees?"

Her face was whiter than its usual pallor. "He sees others, exactly like himself. Duplicates. They swarm over him, but he fights. They cover him with their bodies, but he thrusts them aside—"

Cafter cried out and crumbled to the floor. Tourmaline knelt at his side and fumbled with a wrist.

"Is he dead?" said Obregon.

"I don't know. How do you tell with a simulacrum?"

"Jade Blue," said Terminex.

The catmother crouched close to the floor and

snarled defiantly. After a moment the growl trailed off. Obregon looked questioningly at Torre.

"She is fighting for her kittens."

The catmother lurched and slowly rolled onto her side. She lay still. "Jade Blue!" Tourmaline cried.

"Torre," Terminex said.

"Wait," Obregon said, "this is going too fast."

Torre too crumpled; but before she struck the floor she vanished with a pop of displaced air.

Tourmaline Hayes," said the computer inexorably.

Tourmaline looked momentarily at Obregon, then resolutely faced the primal metal egg that was Terminex. After a few seconds she collapsed upon the floor of the chamber. Obregon stared down at the litter of bodies, his fists white-knuckled.

"Is something the matter, Timnath?" said the computer. "Is all this progressing too rapidly for your vaunted intellectual prowess to digest?"

Without thinking, Obregon launched himself at the metal ovoid. As his fingers closed about the slick surface of the computer, it occurred to him that he was not yet being stopped by Terminex. No force field, no enchantments, no tractor beams, no defenses at all were in evidence. And then with a burst of hysterical strength he hurled the computer from him; in a perfect trajectory, Terminex hurtled toward the anomaly.

"What is this, Timnath? So frail and human an analogue to a thinking machine such as I, junking your cool rationalism and lashing out spontaneously? A noble and desperate gesture . . ." Yet the voice was not entirely mocking.

To Obregon's eye, the ovoid appeared to fall slower and slower as it approached the ebony lightlessness of the anomaly. Obregon blinked; the metal egg blurred and grew fainter. Then he was rocked back, staggered, felt his back press against the metal wall as a voice spoke in his brain:

Are you again wondering if I am performing irrationally?

Terminex? What—is happening?

For one compressed portion of a moment, you and I have a last opportunity to converse.

What about the others? What did you do to them?

Nothing. They are fine; even Torre.

They don't look fine.

I realize you may have your doubts, but trust me.

Then the test— We passed?

It was a sham. If there were indeed a test, it was met when all of you decided to journey here.

Then why the charade?

To give each of you an opportunity to reconsider your actions and your motives for breaking out of Cinnabar's eternal but stagnant patterns. I was curious to know your respective overriding considerations when pressed into this final confrontation. You may be interested to know that in none of your minds was the city's salvation any sort of direct factor. It was as I had suspected.

What will happen to Cinnabar?

You all will have to get along on your own; the city can no longer care for you. I exaggerated the severity but not the existence of the functional senility damaging me. The time dilation/contraction effects' infinite small impositions on my systemic synchronicity are cumulative. I cannot solve this problem other than by flight.

The inhabitants, can they survive—?

They survived before I existed; certain ones will continue to do so. The city will persevere, even if the populace numbers as few as four.

But—

My decision is firm; my action, irrevocable.

The anomaly—what will happen to you?

I suspect I can enter the other universe only as a collection of subnuclear particles, randomly distributed.

Then you'll die?

Not necessarily. Like certain other organisms, machine-life particles possess a quality you might best compare to imprinted somatic memory. It is possible that in the other universe I will compose a primal seed of matter and energy. Altered somewhat, I may survive.

In a computer universe ...

It is conceivable.

I wish you luck, Terminex.

The moment of compression ends. Timnath, I offer you good-bye and good fortune.

Obregon blinked again as the voice was swallowed by the anomaly. The image of the ovoid blurred to infinite faintness. The scientist dropped to his knees; the bodies sprawled around him stirred with movements and small sounds of discomfort. "Tourmaline? Jade Blue?"

"Oooh. My head aches." Tourmaline sat up unsteadily and took Obregon's hand for support. "Is Terminex—?"

"Gone? Yes, forever."

She smiled shakily. "Timnath, you're a wizard."

"Me?" Obregon said. "Hardly. Let Terminex be the last wizard."

"And so it was," said Jade Blue. "Look about us."

Obregon noticed then that the smooth, cold metal of the domed chamber had been replaced by gravel chips. He slowly arose and then helped Tourmaline to her feet. They stood in a desolate wasteland.

Rubbing his temples, Cafter faced them. "Look behind you," he said. "Terminex saved us a long walk."

They turned and saw the city in the distance. "See there?" said Jade Blue, indicating. "Smoke."

"It appears as though Craterside Park is burning," said Cafter, "as well as other districts."

For a moment there was no sound, no movement among them as they stared at one another.

"Let's go home," Obregon said.

CODA:

It weaves through the warp of the desert; a dusty trail looping around wind-eroded buttes, over dry stream beds, among clumps of gray scrub brush. Straighter, but always within sight of the roadway, is the elevated train track. No trains have run in centuries and the track is streaked with verdigris. Though there are seldom travelers to hear it, the wind in the trestles shrills atonal scherzos.

Closer to the city, the road is lined with the burned-out shells of what were once buses.

Then comes the greenbelt, a mile-wide sward of grass and trees no longer tended by small silent machines.

At last, the city. Cinnabar is a flux of glass towers and metal walls perched atop red cliffs crumbling down to a narrow band of beach and then to ocean.

The desert. The greenbelt. The city. The sea. There seems very little more to the world. The elevated railroad is rumored to run to a place called Els. But no one is quite sure; no one remembers ever having traveled so far.

Today a quartet trudges along the road to Cinnabar. (Once there had been five: but elsewhere and elsewhen a singularity divulges a point; and that point generates a line; and the line generates a plane, which rotates into a solid and there you are, Torre.)

First, Jade Blue. She knows with utter sureness that a litter of kittens, safe and real, awaits her in the city.

Second, Cafter. He has earned his own individualness; been given uniqueness. He knows he is his own . . . man.

Third, Tourmaline. Another adventure completed. But with the accumulation of sensation, something more lasting is catalogued. She has not yet divulged to Obregon the singular insight she stripped away and confronted at the computer's urging.

Fourth, Obregon. He has gathered the information

he desired, but has as well discovered a synergistic conclusion greater than the sum of his inputs: he possesses heart as well as mind.

A catmother and a simulacrum and a woman and a man, they approach the city. Dying Cinnabar waits.

ABOUT THE AUTHOR

EDWARD BRYANT'S speculative fictions have appeared in publications as diverse as *Orbit* and *National Lampoon*, *Again Dangerous Visions* and *Rolling Stone*. He has published one other short story collection, *Among the Dead*. Besides being a writer and editor, he occasionally teaches and lectures. He has a Rocky Mountain inlander's fascination for sharks, and is a novice parachutist.

OUT OF THIS WORLD!

That's the only way to describe Bantam's great series of science-fiction classics. These space-age thrillers are filled with terror, fancy and adventure and written by America's most renowned writers of science fiction. Welcome to outer space and have a good trip!